Gun watched Eva arrange the bedrolls side by side on the floor. As she bent over, the weight of her breasts hinted through her blouse.

"Putting them a little close, aren't you?" he asked, referring to the bedrolls.

"I'm scared."

"Scared of what?"

"Snakes, scorpions, tarantulas."

Gunn supressed the urge to laugh. "Likely they're just as scared of you," he said, "but, suit yourself. . . ."

Gunn woke to pressure on his leg. Something brushed against his face like a whisp of cobweb. It took a moment to clear his head, but when he felt a hand sliding across his chest, he understood what was going on.

"Eva, go back to your own blankets," he said drily.

"I can't. I'm still scared. I heard something." She squeezed him with her arm, pressing her breasts against his ribs.

"Have you ever had a man before?" Gunn asked gently.

"No, Gunn, never. And I want you, now."

With that, Gunn pulled her to him.

Eva wasn't so scared of the wild after all. . . .

FIRST-RATE ADVENTURES FOR MEN

#10

AN ADULT WESTERN

THE HOTTEST NEW WESTERN SERIES!

HARD BULLETS

GUNN

BY JORY SHERMAN

ZEBRA BOOKS
KENSINGTON PUBLISHING CORP.

ZEBRA BOOKS

are published by

KENSINGTON PUBLISHING CORP.
475 Park Avenue South
New York, N.Y. 10016

Printed in the United States of America

DEDICATION

**For Banjo Billy and
Basket Annie**

The GUNN Series:

#1 — DAWN OF REVENGE
#2 — MEXICAN SHOWDOWN
#3 — DEATH'S HEAD TRAIL
#4 — BLOOD JUSTICE
#5 — WINTER HELL
#6 — DUEL IN PURGATORY
#7 — LAW OF THE ROPE
#8 — APACHE ARROWS
#9 — BOOTHILL BOUNTY
#10 — RENEGADE RIFLES

CHAPTER ONE

The rattler struck without warning.

The man called Gunn saw only the streaking shadow out of the corner of his eye. A shadow boiling out of the brush with a faint *whick* of sound, like a whip lashing out at slow speed. A shadow streaking toward the leg of his horse, unstoppable.

Gunn's hand flew to his pistol, bat-fast.

The horse screamed as the snake's fangs sank deep into its right foreleg, just above the hock.

Buck, a buckskin gelding, reared in fright.

The snake's fangs hooked into the flesh, held the serpent tight as its sac pumped venom into the horse's veins. Squirting the transparent liquid into tissue, muscle, capillaries.

Gunn grabbed the saddle horn with his left hand to keep from sliding back over the cantle. His pistol snugged fast in his hand, useless. The enemy was below, whipping up as Buck clawed the empty air with frantic hoofs.

The rattlesnake's fangs slipped out of their twin holes, spraying deadly venom. The snake hit the ground with a jarring *thunk*.

Buck pitched, then. Rattling down on his forelegs, kicking out with both hind legs. He whirled, fishtailed, bucked as if scratched by a dozen cockleburrs under the saddle. The venom rushed through his bloodstream toward vital organs. The flesh around the wound began to mortify.

Gunn's sweaty hand lost its grip on the saddlehorn. It slipped off as Buck went straight up in the air, all four hooves leaving the ground. Gunn flew out of the saddle on the bounce, somersaulted, came down on his shoulder.

His pistol flew out of his hand. Clattered in the stones and dust.

Pain shot through his shoulder, his arm.

Buck kicked and snorted, turning in bucking, flailing circles. His neck bowed as he tried to bite at the pain in his foreleg. He kicked at air, brush, rock.

The blunt-nosed rattler, pale yellow eyes glittering, slithered away from the bucking horse. Its forked tongue quivered, flicked in and out of its closed mouth. It stopped, coiled itself to strike again.

Its rattle whirred ominously.

Gunn moved only his eyes. Saw the rattler, ten feet away.

The snake stared at him with cold yellow eyes. Its forked tongue flickered dangerously, seeking the man's scent, his body heat.

Gunn's pale gray eyes fixed on his pistol.

It lay, four feet away, between him and the ominously buzzing rattler.

Gunn moved slightly.

The rattler's head raised, silent as smoke.

8

Buck's legs caved in and he sank to the ground, kneeling on his forelegs.

Bile rose in Gunn's throat. He fought the sickness down.

Buck was dying!

The rattler flinched slightly when the horse moved. Gunn's eyes swept back to it. He judged the snake to be about four and a half feet long. He couldn't count the rattles, but he figured more than a dozen plus the button. The snake was a diamondback. It could move fast and strike like lightning.

Gunn gazed into the serpent's yellow eyes, slitted by a vertical black line.

Buck made a sound, tried to struggle to his feet.

The horse's eyes rolled in their flared sockets. His breath was a grating rasp. Gunn saw that the animal was suffocating. He winced. This was the second buckskin he had owned since . . . since Laurie's death. He had had to shoot the first one. He would have to shoot this one too. He would own no more pale horses. This would be the last Buck he would own.

The rippling muscles under the horse's hide were turning to stone. Buck sank to his side, other muscles twitching. Gunn could almost see the poison spreading through the horse's massive system. Slowly turning him into a helpless hulk.

Gunn had to reach the pistol.

He knew that if he made one mistake he was a goner.

The snake's head snapped back into its coils. Tongue flicking. Eyes vacuous, glittery as tiny yellow marbles.

Could the snake hit him from that distance?

Probably.

It would be close. Too close.

Gunn stretched out a hand. Slow as he could manage. Forcing the slowness, holding his breath. Watching the rattler.

The snake's head moved slightly, bobbed down behind the coils. Stared at the man without blinking with ice-cold slitted eyes.

The hackles rose on the back of Gunn's neck.

He withdrew his hand.

The snake continued to rattle.

Brrrrrrrrrrrrrrrrrrrr!

Buck thrashed in mortal agony. The horse stiffened, his muscles contracting, spasming as the venom surged through his veins. Attacked the nerves, crippled the vital organs, arrowed toward his heart and his brain.

The snake was distracted by the horse's movement.

Gunn could wait no longer. The snake was sure to strike. Any minute. Any second.

He drew a deep breath, dug his toes into the hard ground. He flung himself forward, pushing with his legs.

His hand lashed out for the pistol.

The rattlesnake struck!

Hurtling across eight feet of no man's land, the rattler was a blurring whip in the air, its hissing like the snicking sizzle of an Apache arrow. A second's tick of time was an eternity. Gunn felt he was moving in slow motion while the snake flew toward him at the speed of light itself.

Gunn's hand closed around the pistol butt.

He jerked the weapon up, hammering back with his thumb.

The snake landed a half a foot short, writhing in anger, fangs bared, yellow ooze dripping from the hollow points.

Gunn triggered the Colt .44, aiming instinctively. He saw the blunt snout of the snake just over the blade front sight.

The .44 bucked in his hand.

White smoke and flame belched from the muzzle of the barrel.

The snake's head flew off its body with a loud *pop,* sailed twenty feet through the air. It struck the ground, bounced like a skipping stone into the brush.

Gunn stared at the twitching, undulating body of the beheaded reptile. The scales twitched spasmodically. The diamond patterns rippled with life.

Sweat soaked his brows, poured into his eyes.

Gunn scrambled to his feet, shaking inside. There might still be time to save Buck. He rammed the Colt into its holster and drew his Mexican knife. The blade gleamed silver in the sun. The dull brass of the eagle's head jutted from the antler-inlaid handle. He grasped it tightly, gritting his teeth at what he had to do.

"Steady, Buck," he said, kneeling beside the stricken animal. He put a hand on the horse's neck, lifted the foreleg with the twin holes oozing blood and clear yellow fluid.

Buck made a sound. His eyes were glazed, constricted in pain. His breathing was shallow, raspy.

Gunn made a quick slash just above the wound where the swelling was worst. Yellowish, pus-like fluid gushed out, mingled with a dark thin stream of blood. Gunn dropped his knife in the dirt. He then untied the bandanna around his neck, wrapped it around the top of the leg. He twisted it tightly, cutting off the flow of poison. Even as he did this, he knew it was too late.

He looked again at Buck's eyes, winced.

Gunn slid the knife back in its sheath, took a deep breath.

"Sorry, boy," he husked, drawing his pistol.

He thumbed the hammer back, put the pistol to the horse's skull. Squeezed the trigger. The noise was deafening. Flame and hot lead burst from the barrel. Buck's brain exploded. The force of the bullet blew Buck's head sideways. The big animal shivered, convulsed, and rolled into a still hulk. He did not breathe again.

The snake's headless body twitched, drawing Gunn's attention to it.

He whirled, anger hardening his jaw. He hammered back as he bent to a natural crouch. He fired, fanning the hammer, fired the remaining bullets into the writhing snake. The bullets shredded the diamonds, split the skin, gouged out chunks of veined meat.

Gunn's curses filled the air, rang in counterpoint to the rapid explosions. His arm went slack, the pistol drooping to his side. He stood up straight, stunned by the sudden silence, the shock of his own anger unleashed at something that was already dead.

It took him a quarter hour to strip Buck of saddle, bridle, saddle bags. Buzzards circled in the sky overhead as Gunn slung the gear over his shoulder and started out on foot toward Tres Piedras. He hoped to buy a horse there and ride on to Taos. He was south of Tierra-Amarilla in the wild high country where it was cool in that late summer. Still, he started to sweat under his buckskin shirt and the saddle gained weight as he walked down the middle of the trail.

A roadrunner dashed across the trail at one point, startling him as it came up from behind. He turned and saw the reason the bird had taken that course. Behind him, a wagon rumbled up the road, pulled by a single dray horse. Gunn set his saddle down beside the road and waited. The clank and clatter increased as the wagon drew nearer. The horse wore blinders and the man on the seat hunched under the shade of a floppy sombrero.

The wagon jolted to a stop next to the place where Gunn stood.

The man at the reins was prematurely balding, appeared to be in his early forties. He pushed back the floppy sombrero as he set the brake, reached into his shirt pocket for the makings. His face was browned by the sun and wind, his dark eyes framed by the deep furrows of crow's feet. He had some teeth missing and whistled as he spoke through cracked dry lips.

"Your hoss back there?"

Gunn nodded.

"Snake bit, eh?

"Snake bit. The name's Gunn. You goin' to Tres Piedras? This saddle's a mite heavy."

"Smoke? My handle's Morgan. Ethan Morgan out of Santy Fe."

Gunn didn't want a smoke. He shook his head.

"Throw your saddle in the back can ye find room. Climb up here on the seat. We'll set a spell, let Dobby catch his breath."

The horse's ears perked at his name. His tail flicked at invisible insects.

The wagon was loaded with trade goods, boxes, tarp-covered cartons. The wagon was a flatbed, with side panels made of colorful cloth. Pots and pans hung from the posts. Gunn didn't know how a man could ride with so much din. The wagon carried a lot of weight, besides.

Gunn climbed up on the seat, glad to have his saddlebags and tack aboard.

"Had to shoot your hoss, eh?" He built the cigarette quickly, lit it.

"I did."

"Don't do a man no good to shoot his hoss. First time?"

"No." It wasn't. He'd owned another buckskin with the same name. The horse had caught a load of double ought buck and had to be destroyed. It was the toughest thing a man had to do. A man got used to a horse, depended on one for a lot when he rode lonely miles in strange country. Both Bucks had been good horses.

Ethan Morgan flipped his hat back down, drew deeply on his cigarette.

"You going to Tres Piedras?" Gunn asked again.

"And beyond. To Taos. It's August, son, and they's the fair."

"The fair?"

"Ever' August. Folks from all over come to the pueblo to trade goods, barter trinkets, get sozzled, whack a few backs and dance with the purty gals."

Ethan kicked the brake free and took up the reins. He clucked to Dobby, and the horse strained against the traces. The wagon moved, wood groaning under the weight.

14

"We got to wait up yonder though. 'Nother wagon follerin'."

"Yeah?"

"They's a *hueco* up ahead where we can water Dobby and the mules. She'll be comin' along directly. Them mules is slow and blinkered to keep 'em quiet. Mean bastids. But she kin handle 'em. Fact is, she's the only one who can."

"She?"

"You don't talk much do ye, son? Just ask durn fool questions." Morgan spat out of the side of his mouth. Gunn noticed the draw end of the cigarette was soaked through with spittle.

Gunn didn't say anything.

"Daughter bringin' up the wagon a ways behind me. She's no more'n a pup-kid, but smart as a whipsnake. Pore little Eva, she took hit hard when her ma passed on. My woman took sick two year ago down to Santy Fe. Come down with the fever."

Morgan looked at Gunn for sympathy. Looked into eyes gray as a winter sky. Scanned the hard jawline, the bent nose, the full sensuous lips. Raked the dusty buckskins, the wide shoulders, the broad chest. A man sat next to him, holding a Winchester .44-.40 and there was no sign he had any feelings whatsoever. A chill went up Morgan's spine and he looked away.

"What're you hauling, Morgan?" Gunn asked.

Morgan's right hand slipped down the reins toward his holstered pistol. Cigarette smoke stung his eyes, but he ignored the tears.

"Ordnance," said Morgan, a gruff tone to his voice.

"Guns?"

Morgan slipped his pistol free of the holster. He

moved slowly, his right side concealed from his passenger.

"That's right, son."

Gunn heard the click of the hammer being eased back. He looked at Morgan, startled. Morgan whirled, leveling the pistol at Gunn's head.

"What the hell. . . ." Gunn started to say.

"You twitch an eye, move a finger and I'll blow you out of the seat," gruffed Morgan

Gunn's eyes narrowed. He stared into the black hole of the barrel.

Stared at death as Morgan's finger curled around the trigger.

A second went by.

Then another.

Morgan seemed to be trying to make up his mind. His hand was steady, his eyes fixed on Gunn's. The wagon rumbled along, bouncing the two men on the seat. But the pistol in Morgan's hand went up and down with the rhythm of the wagon. More seconds passed.

Gunn saw Morgan's finger move on the trigger. Another second slid by.

And suddenly there were no more seconds left.

CHAPTER TWO

"You damn fool!" Gunn said. "You think I'm a damned highwayman? Put that gun down!"

Gunn bunched his muscles to spring at Morgan if the man's finger moved again. His eyes held steady, not betraying his intention.

Morgan relaxed for an instant. His trigger finger went slack. That was enough for Gunn.

He moved, dropping his rifle to the floor of the seat.

Springing forward, he clawed at Morgan's face with his left hand. His right hand swatted at the barrel of the pistol aimed at his head.

The explosion almost tore off Gunn's head.

Powder burned his face. The roar deafened him. His fingers dug into Morgan's cheekbone, drew gouts of blood.

Morgan screamed, tried to hammer Gunn down with the pistol.

Gunn bulled forward, flailing Morgan with his right fist. The reins fell out of Morgan's hand as he tumbled backwards. The two men fell from the wagon, Morgan still clutching his pistol. They landed in a cloud of dust, bouncing to a stop. Morgan tried to sit up, bring his pistol around to fire again. Gunn lashed out with a boot, struck the man square in the groin. Morgan doubled over, howling in pain and rage.

"Drop that pistol or I'll snap your wrist in two!" Gunn ordered.

Morgan swung the pistol toward Gunn.

"Dammit, man!" Gunn yelled, then laid a fist smack into Morgan's jawbone. Morgan's body went slack. His eyes rolled and he slid down on his back, the pistol falling from lifeless fingers. Gunn picked up the pistol, tossed it into the wagon. He puffed for breath, standing over the unconscious man.

When he regained his breath, he hefted Morgan up by the shoulders, hauled him to the wagon. He rolled him into the seat, climbed over him to take up the reins. He hollered to the horse and rattled the reins. The wagon lumbered off, Morgan a dead weight on the seat, rolling and pitching with the motion.

Gunn reached over and moved the sawed-off shotgun to his side of the wagon. Morgan might be fighting mad when he woke up. He kicked the pistol under his feet, out of the conked-out man's reach.

Moans told him that Morgan was regaining consciousness.

Gunn tensed, his hand near his pistol. He'd have to put the old man away again if he woke up ornery.

"What the hell . . ." groaned Morgan, rubbing his head. He tried to lift it, grimaced in pain.

"You hadn't ought to draw on a man with no reason," Gunn said quietly. "I mean you no harm. You spook too easy, I reckon. Sit up slow and get your bearings. I don't bear you no grudge if you don't jump

18

to any more conclusions.

Morgan sat up, felt his face with trembling fingers.

"You pack a mean wallop, Gunn. My lights went out for fair and I figger you coulda done me in back there."

"At least I'd a had a reason."

Morgan groaned, more from self-anger than pain. He moved his head in a circle, tilting it backwards slightly, as if to reassure himself that it was still attached to his shoulders.

"I had that coming. Heard you askin' about my wares and I thought I'd been suckered. My mistake."

"You're crazy as hell to haul guns in this country, Morgan. There's more bandits to the square foot in this god-forsaken country than any place besides Kansas or the District of Columbia.

Morgan flashed a weak grin.

"You're right, o' course. I see you're totin' a Winchester .44-.40. Fine rifle, mind you, but until you've shot a Sharps' Model 1874 with a combination sight, you hain't held a weapon. Why, for business or sportin' a Sharps cain't be beat. Forty-five caliber with a hunnert grains of fine black powder, the Sharps Creedmore ca'tridge is some load."

"Little too much gun for a saddle weapon," Gunn observed.

"For that, I got Eli Whitney Junior's patent breech-loading sawed-off double-barrel equalizer."

"You mean this?" Gunn said, hefting the weapon.

"That's the one. It'll cut a man in half at close range. The shot starts to spread two, three inches out of the barrel. Double-ought buck, a dozen to the ca'tridge does some terrible things to a man's flesh."

"You a gunsmith?"

"That's my trade. But I specialize in the Sharps. I also got the greatest buffalo hunting weapon knowed. It's a Sharps too, but made by the Freund Brothers up in Cheyenne."

"I've been to the Wyoming Armory in Cheyenne," said Gunn. "Talked to Frank and George a time or two."

Morgan's face lit up like a sun-kissed peach.

"Then you know their trackside shops. They got 'em all along the Union Pacific. Not only in Cheyenne, but in Laramie, Benton, Green River, Bear City, Salt Lake and the Terminus."

"They sold most of them off I heard."

"Yep," said Morgan, slapping his knee in delight. He had finally found someone to talk to and his face continued to beam. "They still got a big shop in Denver and the Armory. That's where I buy my Freund Sharps. I sell a heap of 'em to buffalo hunters."

"Not in Taos."

"No, up north. Quickest way to drive out the Indians, says the government. You ever shoot one of those rifles?"

Gunn shook his head.

"Powerful. Accurate as any. Single-shot, come in all calibers. But the best is the fifty-caliber. Shoot a lead ball what weighs about an ounce. Can take a buff at eight hunnert yards or more. Deadly on the toughest bulls at three hunnert yards."

"I don't hold with hide hunters."

"Never you mind. They's here and they ain't the onliest ones who uses the Freund Sharps. Eddy Street is swarmin' with soldiers, railroad men, cowboys and teamsters, all heading north after gold. They like the big rifles."

"They'll ruin the country and lose some scalps, I reckon." Gunn knew the Sioux wouldn't be able to hold onto the Black Hills now that Custer had spread the word about gold in the sacred land. It was sad. But Morgan was right. They were there, the white men, and their numbers grew every day. Every year.

"This'll be a big year up north for the Freund. The Sharps is here to stay."

"So is the Winchester," Gunn said, patting the barrel of his rifle.

"There's the *hueco* up ahead," Morgan said, pointing. "Turn left, up the hill."

"We'll wait for your daughter there, I reckon. Aren't you worried about her?"

"Eva? She can take keer of herself, son."

Gunn pictured a gangly youngster of thirteen or fourteen driving a wagon full of guns and ammunition through territory that teemed with highwaymen of every sordid ilk. Now that he knew what the wagons carried, he was nervous himself. Even though Morgan didn't seem to be worried about his daughter, Gunn wasn't so sure that they were safe. The *hueco* was a natural, hollowed-out flat rock that was filled with water. He scanned the low-lying hills, the mesas and buttes in the distance. He looked over every nearby clump of sage, every Saguaro, each barrel cactus to make sure they weren't being watched. Ethan Morgan didn't seem at all worried now, yet he had almost shot him dead when he thought Gunn was a bandit. He decided that Morgan was one of those who worried about the wrong things at the wrong time. He was almost carefree as he jumped out of the wagon and started stripping off the horse's blinders and bridle so that the animal could drink.

"You want this, Morgan?" Gunn tossed the gunsmith's pistol to him. Morgan caught it deftly in mid-air.

"Nobody's been here," said Morgan. "Not recent. No cause to worry."

"You were worried about me."

"Hell, I was minded of a tale told me last year when we come to Taos. Man stopped to help another man on foot and a whole passel of Mexican bandits rode up out of the brush and stripped the man clean. He was a drummer carrying whiskey. Beat him to a purple pulp."

"Yeah, well you got an imagination all right. Man don't carry a saddle with him when he's in the ambush business."

Morgan winced. Gunn was sorry now that he had criticized the man. Morgan meant well. He just thought like a shopkeeper. One hand on his moneybag, the other on his pistol.

Gunn stepped down and leaned against a rock above the *hueco*. He built a smoke, rolling it tight, lit it with a sulphur match. He kept the Winchester handy. Morgan was right about no one having been to the *hueco* recently, but that only made Gunn more suspicious. It wasn't natural that the water hole hadn't been used. Someone could be watching them at that very moment.

Morgan, he was sure, was an ambush just waiting to happen.

Gunn heard the other wagon before Morgan did.

He looked up, saw it top the rise. He squinted into the western sun.

Eva Morgan was not the gangly, pimple-faced girl he had expected.

She was not what he had expected at all.

She drove up, clucking to a span of mules with blinkers on, pulled them to a halt beside her father's wagon.

When she stood up, the sunlight shone through her hair. Light brown hair that turned copper as the sun struck it from behind. She was about nineteen, he figured, with fair skin that had been tanned by sun and wind. She had large dark eyes. As she stepped down, he saw a flash of ankle. She was tall and willowy, graceful as a female cougar. She walked to the team and he noted the femininity that marked her movements despite the trousers and shirt she wore. Her hair was swept up and he saw the light streak where she had worn a hat. Probably to give the casual observer the impression that she was a boy. But her breasts were much too developed to foster that impression for long. They strained against the checkered shirt she wore, tugged at the button that held fast just below the lower halves of her breasts.

Gunn blew a spool of smoke into the air, sucked in a breath.

Eva looked up at him, then at her father. Her eyebrows arched in a questioning look.

Ethan walked over to her and spoke in low tones. Gunn couldn't hear what was being said, but he saw Eva touch her father's jaw. She shot a sharp dark look in his direction. He stubbed out his cigarette on a flat stone and sat there watching the two, not wishing to intrude on their private conversation.

Ethan unhitched the mules, led them to the *hueco* to drink. Eva let her hair down. It was long and cascaded down her back, reaching a point just above her hips. Her back was turned to Gunn. She walked to the back of her wagon, the larger of the two, and disappeared inside. Gunn stood up, sauntered down to the *hueco*.

"She don't like me much, does she?" Gunn asked.

"Eva's right shy around strangers. Men, especially."

"I'll stay clear of her 'til we get to the next town."

"Oh, Eva will come around. I told her what happened. How it was my fault and all."

"She believe you?"

"Course. I'm her pa."

The mules made bubbling and slurping noises. The horse, full, had wandered off on hobbles to seek nonexistent shade. Gunn didn't like the spot at all. The watering place sat in a bowl-like depression with ground sloping toward it. He felt hemmed in, unable to see for more than a hundred yards in any direction. The main road passed below the *hueco,* was obscured by cactus and salt cedar, some stunted pines. There were a lot of game tracks in the soft earth, but these too, were days old. There was little water in the *hueco* when the pair of mules finished drinking. The sun was falling over the horizon. It would be dark in an hour and a half.

Gunn helped Ethan hobble the mules, against his better judgment.

"Be better if we found some other place to spend the night," he said.

"Some place of your own choosing, no doubt!"

Gunn spun around, saw Eva standing six paces away, a defiant look hardening her face. She wore a sidearm now and her long hair had been brushed to a coppery sheen. She smelled of fragrance, too.

"Some place high," Gunn said quietly.

"Settle down, Eva," said Ethan, stepping up to come between the two. "This here's Gunn and I think he's right square."

"Yeah? He probably killed his horse deliberately so's he could get at the rifles. I wouldn't trust him far as I could throw that wagon yonder."

"You saw my horse back there," Gunn said. "It was snake bit."

"I didn't notice," she humphed. "Just keep away from them wagons, stranger, or I'll gun you down."

Gunn stepped back in surprise as Eva made a smooth draw. She did not, however, hammer back. The pistol was a Colt's Mason-Richards conversion of the .44 cap-and-ball Army. Plenty of gun for a man, much less a young woman. This pistol was worth about twelve dollars new and used centerfire ammunition.

"Don't worry, ma'am," Gunn told her. "I'll not go near your wagons. I'll buy me another horse in Tres Piedras tomorrow and be on my way. I'm not after your rifles."

Eva snorted and holstered the big pistol. She stalked off. Gunn looked at Ethan and shrugged.

"Independent little cuss," Morgan said, an admiring tone in his voice.

"Pretty as a desert flower," Gunn said under his breath. "And just as thorny, too."

"Huh? You say somethin'?"

"You still aim to camp here, Morgan?"

"Just as well. Water here for the mornin'. We can get a good start come sun-up."

"It's about the worst place I can think of. Probably the only watering hole in forty mile and locked in here where a man can't see thirty yards in any direction. We ought to get to high ground like I said, off the trail. We can ride back this way after we break camp."

Eva overheard Gunn's plea and came back at him.

"Well, I'm plumb tired, Mister Gunn," she snapped, "and if Pa says we camp here, we camp here! You don't like it, you can just keep walkin'!"

Gunn suppressed a smile.

Eva had fire, defiance, beauty.

He put up both hands in mock surrender.

"All right, missy, back down," he said. "Peace?"

"Humph! Get some wood and make me a fire, you two, or you'll eat cold hardtack for supper!"

Eva whirled and left the two men standing there with sheepish looks on their faces. A moment later they heard the rattle and bang of pots and pans from inside her wagon.

The meal was better than Gunn had expected: a stew with potatoes and wild onions, beans that hadn't been burnt, beef that didn't tear out your teeth when you chewed it down, hot strong coffee, fresh biscuits that were as big as saucers. The campfire was comforting as the temperature dropped, but like a beacon, the firelight bouncing off the rocks, the glow could probably be seen in Santa Fe and Taos both. Gunn went to his bedroll uneasy, dogtired. He laid out his rifle and pistol beside him, used his saddlebags for a pillow and went under fast. Eva and Ethan were still up, talking in low voices under the stars, when he lost consciousness.

Sometime later, Gunn was aroused from a deep sleep.

Someone yelled. There were horses screaming. A man cursing. He sat up quickly, reached out for his rifle.

Lights exploded in his brain. He saw nothing but blackness as he sagged back down to his bedroll.

CHAPTER THREE

The throbbing seemed to come from a point just back of Gunn's left ear.

It spread through his head in surging arrows of pain. Big pain. The kind of pain that pumps the blood faster, makes a man afraid to open his eyes.

Gunn opened his eyes.

The morning light was murky, but he couldn't tell whether it was natural or just the way he was seeing things. His head felt as big as a ten-gallon drum. He blinked, saw the sun was just climbing over the horizon and the sky was overcast. He sat up, saw that his rifle and pistol were gone.

His stomach twitched.

Twitched with a sudden pang of fear.

He looked around the camp, despite the pain back of his eyes.

The wagons were gone!

So were the mules and the horse. His rifle and pistol, his saddle. Everything but his bedroll and saddlebags. He snatched the leather packets up, fished out the spare pistol, a Colt .45 centerfire. It was loaded. Five bullets. There was a box of ammunition, a roll of bills, some hardtack, jerky. Nothing had been touched.

He saw why. When he had been hit, he'd fallen over the saddlebags, covering them with his stomach. He felt his face. It was streaked with dirt. He touched the lump on the back of his head. It was soft, tender, caked with dried blood where the skin had been broken.

Gunn stood up on shaky legs, surveyed the camp.

Ethan Morgan's bedroll was empty. He looked at the one next to where Ethan had lain. There was a lump of blankets. He shoved the pistol inside his belt, walked over. All he saw, when he looked down, was a wide-brimmed hat. Over a person's face.

He stooped over, lifted off the hat.

Eva's forehead glistened with a shiny, egg-sized lump. About the same size as the one behind his left ear.

"Eva? Miss Morgan?"

She didn't stir.

He picked her up gently, the blankets falling from her petticoat. She had stripped out of her man's clothing, was barefooted. The white petticoat clung to her body as he carried her over to the *hueco*. He lay her down beside the pool of water. He stripped off the bandanna from around his neck and soaked it in the water. He dabbed at her face, careful not to touch the lump. Eva shivered. Her eyes opened to thin slits, then widened.

She touched her forehead, winced.

"Careful. You've got a nasty lump there."

"Pa? Where's Pa?"

"Gone. So are the wagons, all the gear."

Her face contorted then. Her doe eyes narrowed. She glared at him with undisguised hatred.

"I was right about you! You robbed us! What have you done with my pa?"

She sat up. Gunn backed away.

"Easy girl. I didn't do anything. I'm still here. That ought to tell you something. And I got a lump just like you behind my ear."

"Show me!" she spat.

Gunn ducked down, twisted his neck.

"I don't see anything!

"Put your hand on it. Gentle, now."

She touched him. A shoot of pain plunged through his skull.

"You got a lump, all right." She sat up, then, noticed that she was wearing next to nothing. She crossed her hands over her breasts. "How'd I get here?"

"I carried you over. No need to hide. I've seen women before. Up close, and some not nearly so full-dressed."

"Oh! You!" She scrambled to her feet, ran down the slope of the hillock to her bedroll. She snatched up a blanket, drew it around her. It was still chilly, but Gunn was sorry that her clothes had been in the wagon. She was humiliated, he knew. It would add to her discomfort.

"I'm awful sorry," he said. "Did you see anything?"

"No. Just heard noises and then felt something hit me hard."

Eva reached down, picked up her hat. The crown was crumpled. She put her fist inside, straightened it out, put it on her head.

"That's probably why you're still here. You had that

hat over your face."

"I wear it most of the time. I pulled it over my face last night when I went to sleep."

"If the bandits had known you to be a woman. . . ." He didn't need to say any more. The look on her face told him that she understood. He looked down at his feet, saw that he was still wearing his socks.

He walked back to his bedroll, found his boots under the bottom edge of the soogan. He sat down, put them on while Eva rummaged through her father's bedding as if to search for a clue to his disappearance.

The fire was still smoldering. Gunn cursed. They might as well have advertised all along the trail. Whoever had drygulched them had done it the easy way. Gunn started looking around for sign. He had heard horses. Bandits? Or was it Morgan's horse? Had the men slipped up on foot or just ridden in and taken what they wanted?

After deciphering the maze of tracks, Gunn decided that the bandits had come up to the camp on foot. But they could have seen the three sleepers from above by the firelight. It took him a half an hour to get the rest of the story. When he returned, Eva was slumped over in her blanket, weeping. Her sobs wrenched at him.

"Is—is my father . . . ?"

"He's not here, not up there. No, they took him along. Do you have any idea why?"

Eva shook her head. Her face was streaked with tears, her dark brown eyes red-rimmed.

Gunn put a hand under her armpit, lifted her to her feet.

"We can't stay here. And we can't track the wagons on foot. The bandits lay up there until we were all asleep. Then they just walked down here and started knocking us senseless. Mexicans, I'd say. There's an empty pair of mezcal bottles up the slope and the boots are small-heeled, small-toed. One man is probably an American. Bigger boot tracks, different cut to the leather soles."

"You sound as if you know what you're talking about."

"I've tracked a man or two."

Eva looked into his gray eyes, then looked away quickly.

"You still think I had something to do with this?" he asked.

"I—I don't know. 'I don't have any clothes, any shoes. Pa is gone. I hurt. I—I just don't know!"

"Think you can walk it to Tres Piedras?"

"How far is it?"

"Two days walk at least. I might have to carry you part way."

She drew herself up. "I can walk it by myelf," she said.

"Sure," he grinned. "Come on, then. You can chew on some hardtack and jerky if you're hungry. Grab up your bedroll and I'll get mine. We've got at least one more night in the open."

It was still cool when they set out and the cloud cover held until mid-morning. When the sun shone through and the clouds blew over and broke up, Eva shed her blanket. Gunn helped her roll it into an easier pack to carry. He tried to pick an easy path for her, so that her feet wouldn't blister or be cut to ribbons on the sharp rocks. Still, it was rough going. They managed to average close to four miles an hour. They had no water and he didn't know how far it was to the next water hole. Farther than they could make it on foot, he reasoned.

He began looking up into the hills wondering if he might risk the loss of time to search for water.

"I'm thirsty," Eva said toward noon.

"We'll find a barrel cactus and stop soon," he promised. He had already decided that this would take the least time. Eva might not like the taste, but it would keep her innards from drying out. That was the danger in heat, he knew. That's why he had made sure they both glutted themselves on the water at the *hueco* before they left. Eva had protested, but he'd forced her to drink until she could feel her belly full. Now, he was glad that he had done the same. A white man sipped at his canteen and foundered from heat. An Indian drank all the water he had until his tissues were soaked with it. The white man died from thirst, the Indian went on to find more water.

Gunn spotted a barrel cactus from the trail. It was smaller than most, but his knife was not large enough to slice through a larger one.

The cactus grew next to three saguaros which provided the only shade.

"We'll cut open that cactus and get some rest," Gunn said, taking Eva's arm. When he touched her, he could feel her softness. She was not taking the walk well, physically, but she was brave and determined. He sensed her tiredness, the way she willingly allowed him to lead her. There were rocks and prickly pear barring their way to the barrel cactus.

"Let me carry you," he said. "You'll ruin your feet out there."

"If you want," she said, pooching out her lower lip.

He lifted her easily. She put her arms around his neck, clung to him as he picked his way through the treacherous prickly pear. A man could step on a stick and hurl one into his shin. There would be nothing to do then but to strip out of his trousers and pick out each spine. The holes would be black and blue for a week.

Eva smelled good to him. Her musk was heady in his nostrils. Her hair was sweet-scented, like desert flowers. He felt a breast mashing into his chest. Her legs were solid in the cradle of his arms, her back curved against the other arm.

He set her down gently, on a flat stone just large enough for her buttocks. He drew his knife. Eva looked at it, her brown eyes glittering. The brim of her hat threw shade over her features.

"That's a beautiful knife," she said.

"A gift from a Mexican I knew once."

He showed it to her, let her hold it in her hand. She ran a finger over the brass eagle's head, where the feathers had been etched in, over the inlaid antler that formed the rest of the handle. Her eyes scanned the legend, in Spanish: *No me saques sin razon, ni me guardes sin honor.*

"That's Mexican. What's it mean?"

"Neither draw me without reason, nor keep me without honor."

"Have you ever had to use it—on a man?"

"Yes." He tossed his saddlebags down, turned to the cactus.

She was silent then and he sat down, began sawing on the barrel cactus, careful to avoid the spines. The knife cut only so deep. He cut into the tough meat and drew the knife toward him. It was slow work. He had to take the knife out of the pulp every so often and wipe the sticky fluid on his trousers. He encircled the cactus, cutting as deep as he could. The trick was to cut it just high enough so that the fluid in its center would not drain off. When he had made the slice as clean as he could, he stood up and cocked his leg. He kicked the top of the cactus, aiming so that just his tough heel would come in contact with the spines. The top gave on the first kick. Another kick loosened it further so that he could merely push with his bootheel and snap it off.

He dug into the pulp, cut off a chunk. He handed it, dripping to Eva.

"Chew on this," he said. "It will help."

Gunn began shearing off spines until he'd shaved the bottom part of the cactus in a swath four inches deep. He sliced through this and cut a pie-shaped wedge big enough to shove into his mouth like a piece of pie. He sucked on the moist pulp, felt the moisture trickle down his throat. In the center of the cactus, a pool of slimy fluid had collected. He drew Eva to her feet and showed it to her.

"Drink that, if you can," he told her. "Then we'll carry some of these wedges with us to suck on."

Eva leaned over and slurped. She gagged.

"It's sour," she said.

"It'll keep you from drying out like a prune," he said.

Eva drank some more, then stood up, wiping her lips.

"I—I can't anymore," she said.

35

Gunn finished off the liquid and then cut several more wedges, handed some to her and kept some for himself. He looked at the molten ball of sun in the sky and tried to figure out how many hours of daylight they had left. Too many, but they had to keep moving.

A tarantula skittered out from under a rock and Eva screamed.

Gunn watched it scurry away on feathery legs. He laughed.

"It—it scared me!" she exclaimed.

"Likely you scared him too. Ready?"

She nodded. He lifted her up in his arms again. This time, she clung to him more tightly and watched the ground with keen interest. He set her down on the trail again and as they walked she stayed very close. They scared up a few lizards, a snake or two, but saw no more tarantulas. The landscape was dotted with saguaros, but these were thinning out as they climbed higher.

"They look like trees made by someone who didn't know how to make a tree," Eva observed.

"Someone told me once they were trees turned inside out."

"They are strange."

"The desert is strange," said Gunn, a laconic smile playing on his lips.

Late that afternoon, he crossed the spot where the wagon tracks had come back onto the trail. He stopped, bent down to examine the horses' tracks that accompanied them. Besides the two mules and Ethan's horse, there were tracks of three more horses. The same ones he had seen back at the *hueco*.

"They made a wide loop for some reason and then

came back onto the trail. About three hours ago, I'd say."

"How can you tell?"

"The way the dirt is beginning to fall back into the tracks. You can almost time it, like an hour-glass."

"Where are they going?"

"Same place as we are. Tres Piedras. But they'll get there a lot quicker."

"Darn!" For a moment, Gunn thought she was going to cry, but she was only venting her anger.

"Don't get mad," he said. "Nothing we can do about it. We're afoot and they've got horses. We'll catch up to them in a few days, with luck."

"Don't lie to me, Gunn. We'll never find them in this country." She waved at the desolate landscape.

"Maybe they'll find us."

"Huh?"

"Men know we're looking for them, they just might get nervous. Tracking's not all following."

"Oh, you! Sometimes you don't make good sense."

Gunn kept quiet. The blue skies were now dotted with fluffy cumulus clouds like cottony ships above them. The weather would be fair for a time. He had memorized the tracks of the horses, saw they they were being led behind the two wagons. That meant the men who had jumped them were riding. He wondered if Ethan Morgan was still alive.

"Let's walk faster," said Eva after a while. "Maybe they're up ahead taking a *siesta.*"

"You'd better hope not, girl. They could pick us off at eight hundred yards with those Freund Sharps."

As soon as he'd said it, he knew that Morgan was

alive. And he also knew why the bandits had taken him with them.

Somehow, the theft seemed more ominous than before.

CHAPTER FOUR

Eva stepped up the pace and she had an easier time of it than Gunn. His cattleman's boots were not made for walking and he felt blisters forming on his heels. At one point, Eva was two hundred yards ahead of him, looking back at him mockingly. He knew his blisters would need attention or he'd never make it through another day. They had eaten a pair of cactus wedges before the sun dropped behind a mass of clouds and gave them some relief. By then, it was late afternoon and Gunn had begun looking for a place to camp for the night. The safest place would be off the trail, up in the shelter of the low rocky hills that bordered both sides of the road.

An hour later, the sun was just above the horizon, glinting off the ragged peaks of far mountains. Eva was nowhere in sight as Gunn crested the hill, walking gingerly on tender feet, blistered heels.

He muttered a curse, stopped, scanned the terrain.

Even so, he almost missed it.

A hide cabin, down in a gully off to his right.

And beyond that, a crumbling adobe. His heart

quickened. He shifted the saddlebags to his other shoulder, as he'd done a dozen times that day and continued down the trail.

Now he knew why he hadn't seen Eva. She was waving to him from in front of the hide house.

"Gunn! Down here!" Her voice carried to him, but was broken up by distance so that he had to strain to make out what she said.

He waved back and she disappeared inside the hut again.

Moments later he heard a scream.

Then, Eva burst out of the hide shack, her hat off, hair flying. Her screams hurled icicles in his veins, made the hackles rise on the back of his neck. She ran straight toward him, bare feet scarcely touching the ground. Before Gunn could stop her, she flung herself into his arms. Her last scream needled his eardrums, shattering his senses.

"Hold on," he said as he put his arms around her, mainly to keep her from scratching the hide clean off his face. Her hands flailed at him like clawing windmills.

"There's a rattlesnake in there! It almost got me!"

Gunn started to laugh.

"It isn't funny."

"No," he said soberly, "it isn't. Snake's been the cause of most of my troubles of late."

"Don't just stand there! Go in and kill it!"

"I will, soon as you stop thrashing me within an inch of my life." Her breasts flattened against his chest. Self-conscious all of a sudden, Eva drew away, looked up at Gunn. The terror still glowed in her nut brown eyes. Her face was chalk, her copper hair fell in straggled wisps over her face.

"It liked to scared the life out of me," she explained.

"Hold on, Eva. I'll see if it's still in there."

Gunn stalked past her, approached the hide shack with caution. He drew his pistol from his waistband, tossed his saddlebags down. He stood in the doorway a moment, letting his eyes adjust to the light. It was dark inside. The doorway had been cut from a buffalo hide. There were no windows. It was one of those shacks that men put up in a hurry. They sank logs into the ground, tacked up green buffalo hides, let them cure and draw tight. It made a good temporary shelter. The hair side was turned in to add to the insulation. The underhides were slate black from weathering.

The snake rattled a warning.

Gunn saw it, coiled and waiting, just beyond the door. He saw part of its snout, its blurred tail rattling.

He would have to go inside to take it.

The rattler held its position to the right of the door, just beyond the shaft of light that cut an oblong path through the dark. Now, it had pulled its head back so that Gunn could only see its rattles whirring.

It was now or never. He drew back the hammer of his Colt.

Gunn slid around the door, pistol held belt-high.

The rattles stopped buzzing. Gunn heard a susurrant hiss and saw the dark shape of the snake as it threw itself at him. A piece of black rope in the air. He fired by instinct, hoping the blast itself would blind the snake, cause it to miss. The roar of the .45 was deafening.

Eva screamed again.

Something smacked into Gunn's leg. He felt a rush

of blood to his neck and head. He looked down at the writhing serpent. His hand touched the place where the snake had struck him. He expected to see blood, to feel a sharp pain, then a numbness. Instead, there was no feeling at all. The snake whipped back and forth at his feet as Eva continued to scream hysterically.

"It's killed you! You're going to die!"

Gunn stooped over, his pistol still smoking. He grasped the snake's mantle with his left hand, held it up.

"Missed me!" he grinned, turning to Eva.

Gunn shook the snake to show her that its head was gone.

"Ooooooh! You're not going to die!"

She ran down the slope, pulled up short when she remembered that Gunn still held the snake in his hand.

"Throw that thing away! Please!"

"Make a mighty nice meal."

Eva made a face.

A sound in her throat.

"Trust me," he said, but he tossed the snake a few yards away. He could skin it out, chop it up into steaks later. He ejected the empty shell, slid a fresh one in the chamber. Slid his pistol back in his waistband.

Eva threw her arms around his neck, stood on tip-toes to kiss him. It was a quick kiss, but it was on the lips. He felt his loins stir despite himself. Eva, after all, was clad only in a petticoat and she had enough bare skin showing to get arrested in any town east of the Mississippi.

"Thank you," she breathed, breaking away.

"Step clear. That head's still in there. You step on it

barefooted and. . . ."

Eva blanched again. It took Gunn a little time to poke around and find the head. There wasn't much left of it. It was shredded and smashed. Broken fangs jutting out of pink bloodless flesh. He worried it to the door with the toe of his boot and kicked it outside. Eva jumped when she saw it fly past her.

"Looks like the bandits were in here sometime during the night," Gunn said, scything a thumb toward the door.

"I know. That's why I was excited. Then I heard the rattles and saw the snake. I'm obliged to you for killing it."

"Seems to be just the one. In there for the shade."

"I hope so. There's a lantern inside, and I found something else!" There was excitement in her voice. She seemed eager to show him her find. He followed her inside. The place stank above the mustiness. The smell of dead rodents, stale urine, mezcal. The old and the new.

Eva lit a lantern. The chimney was cracked and smoked up, but the lamp gave off light. There were a pair of wide bunks, a rustic table, a couple of broken chairs, and signs that the recent visitors had eaten of meal of some kind there. Empty cans littered the dirt floor. There were pegs driven into the posts and rusty traps hung from them. A stack of worm and moth-eaten hides were stacked in one corner. Wolf pelts that had probably not graded out good enough to sell.

"They ate goods from our wagon," said Eva, anger shading her voice. "Those were our peaches and beans. There, see, a tin of bully beef I was saving for a good supper."

Someone had put the stove together. The pipe was rusted and Gunn figured smoke would seep through the pinholes that had formed in the tin. But the pipe went through a hole in the roof. The old woodstove was a cheap one, and the firebox was all but rusted out.

"That what you wanted to show me?" he said, pointing to the empty airtights.

"No," she said. "This!"

She reached up on a shelf and pulled down an object. The shelf was covered with a half inch of dust, dead insects, animal hairs and apothecary bottles.

She handed the object to Gunn. It was a carving. A cameo of wood, about the size of a silver dollar. Gunn looked at it, held it close to the smoking lamp. The air reeked of coal oil.

There was the distinct outline of a woman's head. The edges were still rough, but the carving showed some ability. The head was in profile, the cuts deep. The whittle marks were fresh.

"Pretty fair job. Mean anything to you?"

"My father's work. He loves to whittle. He always carves the same thing. That's my mother's portrait."

Gunn's eyebrows went up. He handed the wooden medallion back to Eva.

"You figure he left that up there so's you'd find it?"

"I'm sure of it. He's with them. He's a prisoner. . . ."

"I wonder why," said Gunn. "Seems to me they wanted him alive, but didn't give a damn about us. Were you with him last year when he went to Taos?"

Eva shook her head.

"No, I wanted to come, but he said I wasn't big

enough. He left me in Salt Lake with my aunt."

"Then it could be someone saw him in Taos last year, knew he'd be bringing guns in this year."

"He took a lot of orders for rifles. That's why I got to come along this year."

"You know for sure now I hadn't nothing to do with this,"

"Y — Yes. I — I'm sorry. Real sorry."

Gunn's eyes swept the dark interior of the hide shack. It would do to take shelter there for the night, get an early start in the morning before the heat started to dry out their tissue. He wasn't satisfied with his theory about why Ethen Morgan had been taken prisoner and they had been left alive. At first he had thought maybe Morgan might have followed them on foot, but the tracks didn't bear that out. Then, he wondered. Now, it seemed, he had been taken against his will, but why? Men wanting rifles would just take them, kill all witnesses. Unless there was more to it than just a simple theft. Gunrunners would have just taken them and turned them over for a quick profit.

No, there was something odd about this business. The bandits wanted Ethan Morgan as well as the guns. And Morgan had tried to leave a message for his daughter. What? That he was alive? That he was a prisoner. That, and more.

"Why don;t you scout the land for buffalo chips, wood, or cow pies for a fire. I'll skin out that snake and fix us some steaks. Be better to eat it raw because of the juice, but I reckon you might have trouble keeping it down.

"Yes. I don't know if I can even eat it cooked."

"Just think of it as chicken."

Eva managed to keep the rattlesnake down. Gunn had fried the steaks in lard that he found in the shack. The fry pan was in good shape. There were other utentsils there, too, left behind as if to serve others when the previous occupant moved on.

"Who lived here?" Eva wondered.

"Wolfers most likely. One or two men."

"Wolfers?"

"Trappers working the ranges. Most cattlemen don't hold with using strychnine, so wolfers hire out to rid the range of the worst predators. They use steel traps, deadfalls, snares, rifles. Whatever will do the job. Get so much a scalp, then sell the pelts. It's a good living if a man doesn't mind being alone."

"Do you mind being alone?"

"No."

"Are you married?"

"Not anymore. I was once."

"Did she leave you? Or did you leave her?"

"She was—she died."

"I'm sorry."

"It was a long time ago, Eva."

Gunn walked to the door, looked out at the gathering dusk. The sun had set moments before and the coolness was starting to spread over the land. Eva sat on a bunk, began to ply the top of her head with deft fingers. She separated three strands of hair, gathering each one into a separate length. When this was done, she plaited them into a single braid. She walked to the door, working two hands to cross the strands, draw them tight.

"If I don't do this, my hair will be a mess in the morning. I don't have a comb."

"You have nice hair, Eva."

She drew a deep breath, looked at his keen gray eyes.

"You're different than most men I've seen."

Gunn didn't say anything.

"I mean you're rough, but you're gentle. You look rough. Mean, sometimes. But you've been very patient with me. I didn't like you at first. I thought you were in cahoots with those bandits. Or a bandit yourself. I can see I was wrong."

"You can't always judge by appearances. Did you have trouble with a man?"

"With men, yes. I found them, well, less than honorable."

"All of them?"

"The few I've met. Including my uncle Charlie in Salt Lake."

"Didn't you ever have a beau?"

"A beau?" Eva's laugh was harsh, grating. He looked at her, saw features grow hard. "Since I was twelve, pa has been keepin' me on a short tether. Any boy my own age comes close, he ruffs up like a bantie rooster. Closest thing I had to a boyfriend was Melvin Potter and he was worse than any man. He—he threw me down in the hayloft and tried to take off my underthings. I got away from him, but I wore bruises for near two months."

Gunn stepped outside, found the makings in his pocket. He built a cigarette as the long shadows deepened. A coyote yapped and he heard the call of a wolf from far off. Eva was behind him, but he felt her presence. He didn't know what to say to her. She was a beautiful woman and had probably ripened early. Too early for her to understand the changes inside her.

Men could recognize those changes. Many wanted to be the first to tap the spring. It was not that they were bad men, but they reacted to urges in ways that were puzzling to a young woman. Some were too quick to act on those urges. He could see where they would frighten someone like Eva who had not been exposed to men much.

"Tomorrow we'll be in the high country. Trees. Pines, mostly. It should be cool. There may be water." He looked up and saw the mountains in the distance. "Two hours walking, maybe three."

He found a sulphur match, struck it on his boot. His single-pronged spur gleamed silver in the gathering dusk. The match flared, he touched it to the cigarette, drew deep.

Eva stepped outside, came up to him.

"You don't like me to talk about the men, do you?"

"If it does you any good."

"Are you that way, Gunn? Have you ever forced yourself on a woman?" There was a husk in her voice that made her appealing. He blew a plume of smoke away from her.

"Why do you ask?"

"Curious, I guess. You could force me. We're all alone. I would fight you though. Like a wildcat."

He drew a breath. The cigarette smoke scratched at his throat. He was thirsty. There would be no water until tomorrow. The air was very dry, but at least the cool was coming on.

"Force is no good when you deal with those things

between a man and a woman. If it's forced, it's no good for either one."

"I'm glad you said that," she breathed. "I always knew if it was natural it would be good."

He wanted to move away from her. Change the subject. But her hand touched his arm. It burned through the flesh, burned into his loins.

There were all kinds of force he wanted to say. He felt a force now and it was soft and hidden like the root of a flower taking hold in the earth.

It wasn't always the man who forced "those things" between a man and a woman.

CHAPTER FIVE

The wolf howled again, closer this time.

Eva's fingers tightened on Gunn's arms.

"The wolfers didn't get them all," she said.

"They come back in two or three years. You can't get 'em all. They move on, change their range. They know how to survive."

"Like you. Was she nice? Was she pretty?"

"Who?"

"Your wife. What was her name?"

Gunn drew on the cigarette. The tobacco was staling. Dried out. The smoke scorched his lungs but he held it inside. He didn't want to talk about Laurie. Not now. Not with this girl who was standing so near to him, touching him with fingers of raw fire.

"She was pretty. Her name was Laurie. I loved her."

"I know," she said.

Her hand left his arm and he turned to look at her. Women were a continuing mystery to him. Eva was no less a mystery. With any woman, he knew, it didn't do to take anything for granted. He watched her glide back into the hut, once again, braiding her hair with both hands. A moment later, the doorway flickered with an orange glow. Gunn crushed out his cirgarette, but did not turn to go in. Eva had stirred up something in him. Memories. Memories of Laurie when she was Eva's age. And later, after they had married. Life was big then, and full. They built their ranch in the good rangeland along the Cache le Poudre in Colorado. They raised good beef and they were thinking about starting a family. Then one day all of their dreams were shattered. Men with whiskey on their breaths came and raped Laurie. And someone who thought she was dying shot her. In the back. It was a brutal way to die because the bullet did not kill her right away. She died in his arms without ever knowing who had killed her. In the two years since her death, he had been running, like the lobo that howled in the mountains and on the flatlands. He wondered if he would ever go back to Colorado and look at the land where his life had begun and ended. Wondered if he would ever see the Columbine grow and the aspen turn yellow among the evergreens.

The coyotes were in a pack now, running and yapping, their plaintive yodeling carrying through the still clear air.

The wolf was silent, hunting in his own ancient way as the evening came alive with the creatures that prowled the night after blood and food.

Gunn turned and walked back to the shack. They would probably be safe there for the night. They had some twenty-odd miles to cover, a lot of it hard going through the mountains. But Tres Piedras lay just beyond and part of the walk would be downhill. By tomorrow afternoon they should be there and he could try to find out what happened to Ethan Morgan. He owed the man something. Even though Ethan had later jumped to the wrong conclusions, he had been a Samaritan, picking up Gunn when he had lost his horse and was afoot. Eva was the immediate problem. She was affectionate, but scared. It would be best to keep his distance. His life didn't need further complications just now.

She was finishing off her braid when Gunn walked inside, closed the hide door. He threw up the crossbar, checked it. Solid enough.

Eva reached down and loosened a ribbon on the hem of her pantaloons. Her camisole was partially unbuttoned and he could see the browned curve of a breast as she bent over. She tied the ribbon into a bow at the end of her braid, shook it over her shoulder. Her facial features were sharpened now, enhanced by the flickering glow of the smoking lamp.

As he watched, she lay out the bedrolls, placing them side by side on the dirt floor. She made sure there was nothing underneath to bother them while they slept. Gunn took off his hat, scratched the back of his head.

"Putting them a little close, aren't you?" he asked.

"I'm scared."

"Scared of what?"

"Snakes, scorpions, tarantulas. Rats."

Gunn suppressed the urge to laugh.

"Likely, they're just as scared of you," he said. "But suit yourself. We've an early start to beat the heat."

"It'll be cool in the mountains."

"Don't count on it. We might find where the deer drink if we leave before sunup."

Gunn watched her climb into her bedroll. He pulled off his boots, slipped out of his buckskin shirt. He was aware of Eva watching him with hooded eyes. He left his trousers on, crawled inside his own bedding. Put his pistol under the saddlebags he used for a pillow.

"I'll get the lamp," Eva said, rising up. She blew out the lamp and he heard her rustle across the room in the dark. Saw her white shadow.

Gunn closed his eyes after she was back in bed. He could hear her breathing. He thought she might be as tired as he and go right to sleep. It would ease his mind if she did.

Night sounds filtered into the shack: The yip-yodel of coyotes, the flap of heavy wings, the gruff hoot-hoo-hoo of an owl. The buffalo hides creaked in the cool. A scuttle of claws rattled over a stone. A saguaro sang like a harp in the gentle surge of breeze that rose up from the land.

Gunn woke to pressure on his leg.

Something brushed against his face, like a wisp of cobweb.

A warm bulk next to him.

It took him a moment to clear his head. A hand slid across his chest roiling the wiry hairs. Lips feathered over his cheekbone. Wet, open.

An arm flapped across his chest. He felt a hurried squeeze.

"Eva?"

"Gunn, let me stay here. With you."

Her voice was a soft plea in his ear.

"You can't tempt a man like this."

"I don't care what you do to me."

"I don't want to do anything. Go back to your own blankets."

53

"I can't. I'm still scared. I heard something."

"Can't you sleep?"

She squeezed against him. He felt a breast pressing into his ribs.

"No, not with you here. So close. Gunn, don't turn me away. Make love to me. I want to be a woman with you."

Her scent came to him. Earth, sage, the delicate oils of her sweat.

"Your pa would have my hide."

"No he wouldn't. He wouldn't know."

"Have you ever had a man before?"

"No. Never. I told you. I want you, Gunn. I'm hot all over. Inside."

"It'll pass," he said drily.

She squeezed him with a single arm. Her hand flowed from his chest down to the growing bulge between his legs. Her touch was warm. His loins blazed with a kindled fire.

"It won't pass. I don't want it to. I can feel you. Gunn, I—I hurt inside. Real bad."

He grabbed her roughly, drew her to him. He found her face in the dark, kissed her lips. A shoot of electricity ripped through his spine clear to the groin. He slid his tongue inside her mouth. Into the heat, the moist. Eva responded with her own wet tongue. The heat seared them, melded them together into a twisting mass of desire.

His hand found a breast, slipped inside the camisole. Kneaded its soft spongy bulk, teased the nipple.

Eva writhed in his embrace. Her open mouth enclosed his lips. He felt the hunger, the need, the want.

"Can you get out of your underclothes?" he husked.

"Yes."

He unbuckled his belt, pushed his trousers down. Heard the whisper of cloth as she slipped out of her camisole and pantaloons. He saw a flash of white as she tossed them aside.

She came to him naked, burrowing into him with her hunger.

He took her in his arms, kissed her hard on the mouth. His own hunger rose up to meet hers. His manhood swelled, throbbed with engorged blood. The tip grazed her leg and Eva reached out for it, closed her hand around its swollen length. She squeezed and Gunn felt a spasm wrench his spine.

"This is what I want," she breathed.

"It's yours, Eva."

He rolled her over on her side, attacked her breasts with hands and mouth. His hunger was as deep as hers. Eva was a pliant, willing woman, vibrant with life. She squirmed when he took a nipple in his mouth, worried the tip with his tongue. Her hand tugged on his manhood, moving up and down its length, squeezing it. A sensation of pleasure surged through his loins.

"I can't stand it any more," she moaned. "I want you inside."

She was quick. He eased her under him, spread her legs wide. She released her grip on his pulsing cock. He dipped to her, touched the furred portal of her sex. She bucked with a sudden spasm.

Gunn slid inside, felt the moist heat inundate his shaft.

The feeling was exquisite.

He sank deeper, felt her muscles contract. Her legs

widened. Eva opened like a morning flower.

"I love it," she gasped. "I knew it would be special."

"You're sweet," he told her. "Sweet as clover honey."

Her arms pulled him close and she kissed him. Her back arched as he plunged deeper. His swollen member plowed against the barrier of her womanhood. He nudged it gently, stroking slow to test its strength and resilience.

"Can you feel that?" he asked.

"Yes. My maidenhead. Break it for me, please."

"Not yet. Weaken it first, then it won't hurt so much."

"I don't care if it hurts."

She squeezed him with the muscles in her loins. A tingling sensation shot through his thighs. He continued to stroke, gently battering the hymen, pushing at it, tugging it free from its leathery moorings.

Eva gasped with a sudden orgasm as he glided across her love-button.

"Oh! Oh my!" she shrieked. "Gunn!"

"Good?"

"More than good! Lovely,"

She bucked beneath him as he slid across the point of her clitoral shaft. The orgasms came at a rapid rate until she was thrashing mindlessly in his arms. It took all his effort at self-control to keep from plunging through her maidenhead and spurting his seed. But, he held back, letting her enjoy herself, exulting in the quickness of her. She was like a fast Indian pony, all energy and grace. She bucked and squealed, squirmed and writhed. Her hips moved like waves on the sea and then her legs flew up in the air and she screamed with the pleasure of his penetration.

The hymen broke in a rush of blood.

Eva gasped, then spasmed as though galvanized, when Gunn plunged beyond into the pristine cavern beyond. He sank to the mouth of her womb, felt her fingernails dig into his back, rake furrows until the pain was intense, until there wasn't any more pain. He reached down and grasped her buttocks, jerked her hips upward. Sank still deeper until she was thrashing in his grip like an animal in a trap.

"It's so good!" she exclaimed. "You're so good! I can feel you, all of you, so deep inside me I could scream."

"Scream, then," he said, ramming hard and deep.

Eva screamed.

The notes shattered the night and hung in the still close air of the shack.

Then, it was quiet.

Gunn let her hips fall back down on the bedroll.

He stroked her slow and deep, letting the pleasure seep through her loins, the fibres of her sex. The agony of holding back was enormous, but he steeled himself to last until the right moment. The moment when she would beg for him to release his seed.

She twisted beneath him, caught up in the ecstasy of soft throbbing climaxes. They came in spurts, an endless chain of rippling explosions. She gasped and moaned, dug her fingernails into his back. Drew blood. Gunn was scarcely aware of it, for the pain was sweet. At times he felt as if he was swimming stone drunk. At others, he was sure that he was with Laurie again. In the dark he could not see Eva's face, only smell her musk and feel her softness, the cushioning dankness of her loins.

When it came, it came without warning.

The boiling of his seed, the surging. The electric jolt that shattered his thoughts to confetti.

He clutched her back, tried to stay himself.

"Let it come!" she screamed. "I want you to!"

He let it go. He spurted into her, buckling with pleasure. She held him tightly, clamping her legs tight around his. Held him until he was spent, emptied.

"Oh, Gunn," she soothed, "thank you. Thank you for this."

He fell away from her, sated, the exhaustion complete.

"My pleasure," he panted.

"And mine."

Her finger twirled through his hair as she lay beside him, soaked with sweat. He put a hand on her leg, moved it to the matted thatch of hair between her legs. She moved with the pleasure of his touch.

"Wouldn't you like to have a woman sleeping with you every night?" she asked, after a while, her voice a faint husky whisper.

Gunn took in a breath.

"Yes," he said, "it's nice to have a woman sleeping with you every night. It's nice to know her body. Nice to see it, touch it. Explore the country of a woman. It's an endless country."

"You must miss her a lot."

"Huh?"

"Your wife. Laurie? Was that her name?"

"Laurie. Yes, I miss her. I miss having someone next to me at night who gives a damn if I'm breathing or not."

"I know the feeling. I've never been with a man

before, but I imagined it in my mind. I knew it would be just like this. I feel safe. I feel warm. I'm not afraid anymore. It's like being with God."

"You say it pretty fine."

"Laurie must have loved you. A lot of women must have. Why have you not found anyone else?"

"I'm a wolf, Eva. An untamed wolf. Laurie tamed me once. She let me lay at her feet like a tame dog. She petted me. I liked that. I didn't like being wild too much because it's hard to come into towns and be civil when you've been running free."

"She must have been a smart woman. Your Laurie."

"She was smart about a lot of things. Smart about me. She knew she wasn't the first and probably wouldn't be the last. But I was faithful to her when she was alive. She knew how to keep me tame."

"I wonder if any other woman does."

"A woman has more sense about a man than any man does about himself, Eva."

Eva didn't say anything for a long time. He could hear her breathing, feel her finger worming through his hair. In the darkness, she could have been anyone. Any woman. She had made him full and he was grateful.

Finally, she rolled over so that her breast was mashed against his chest.

She ran her tongue inside his ear. The hackles rose on the back of his neck.

"I want you again," she said. "I want to see if you're still wild."

He took her in his arms.

He was still wild as any wolf.

And so was Eva.

CHAPTER SIX

Tres Piedras basked in the afternoon sun, a sleepy town of adobes and sod houses, at the foot of the mountains. A dog barked and then whined as if someone had given it a sudden kick. A rooster crowed and then was silent.

Gunn saw no sign of movement.

Coming down out of the trees, he and Eva stopped in wonderment. Their throats were dry and their bodies were laced with rivulets of sweat. They had found water that morning, but there was no way to carry any of it with them. The sun boiled through the trees, but they kept on, knowing that if they stopped they might not get up. The heat drained them of energy, sucked out their juices until they felt hollow, emaciated.

"Siesta time," Gunn croaked, his voice alien to him. His throat was parched. The words were formed from rasping files sliding across his vocal cords.

"Let's just get some water," wheezed Eva.

He grabbed her hand, squeezed it.

The last hundred yards was the hardest. A small

Mexican boy, naked, streaked with dirt, stared at them and then ran screaming to his mother.

People came out of the adobes to stare at them.

Gunn stopped at the first house.

"Agua," he said and a young girl brought a dipper full of water.

Gunn gave it to Eva. She drank it hoggishly and then blushed with shame.

"I'm sorry," she gasped. "I couldn't help myself. My throat was on fire."

"Mas agua, por favor," Gunn told the girl.

She ran inside the adobe and returned a moment later, water sloshing out of the dipper. Gunn drank it slow, letting the cool water seep down his throat. Eva clutched her stomach, doubled over in pain.

"You drank too fast," Gunn said. "It'll hurt for a few minutes."

Gunn gave the girl a silver dollar. She whisked away quickly as if afraid that he would change his mind.

Gunn laughed, grabbed Eva's arm.

"Come on," he said, "the walk will straighten you out."

Eva recovered quickly, followed after Gunn who seemed to have renewed strength after drinking a single dipper of water. Eva hung on to her bedroll with effort while Gunn seemed not to notice his own bedroll and the sopping saddlebags slung over his damp shoulder.

They walked down the main street, which was only a continuation of the trail. Tres Piedras boasted a half dozen *cantinas*, a grim stage stop, a dry goods store, mercantile, livery and a hotel. The smell of cooked maize hung in the air along with the sweet aroma of *tepache* and the metallic taste of *mezcal*.

Eyes followed them. Eyes that were peering out of shadows, from behind windows, doors. Gunn felt the stares. They must make a sight: he, wobbling along on blistered heels, Eva, barefoot, her long pigtail slapping against her back, wearing nothing but pantaloons and camisole. An odd pair in an odd town.

The hotel was flanked by *cantinas*. One was called *La Copa de Oro*. The other was *El Saguaro*. The hotel bore a Spanish name as well: *Casa del Sol*. Apt enough, Gunn thought. The sun hammered at the town mercilessly.

"You want to get a room, take a bath, while I get us some horses, try to find out what happened to your pa?"

"A bath . . ."

"I won't be long."

"Gunn, would you get me a pistol? I'll pay you back."

"A pistol? You know how to use one?"

"I surely do. Small caliber. Anything."

There was a light in her eyes he had never seen before. A glitter that was there and then disappeared. There were things about Eva he did not know, would never know. He nodded, pressed some bills in her hand.

"Get us a big room or two small ones close together," he said. "Can you handle it?"

"I'll do it. A bath. I'll soak for an hour."

Gunn laughed, but he saw the hard faces of men at the doors to the cantinas. Saw them out of the corner of his eye. He handed her his bedroll and kept the saddlebags. His money was inside them. He watched her go into the dark doorway of the hotel, shot a glance at the men standing in the shade of the overhang at *El Saguaro*. They looked away from him quickly. Others, at the *Copa de Oro* went back inside when he looked at them. They were all heavily armed and made his scalp prickle.

Gunn stalked to the livery stable. The paint on the false front proclaimed its owner as one J. Cardona.

It was dark inside, musty, reeking of horse hair, droppings, sweat and grain. There was old hay stacked in piles here and there, even older straw in the stalls. A horse snorted. Another one whinnied. Saddles and bridles hung from wall pegs and on the stall walls.

"Anybody here?" Gunn called, through the gloom. He isolated the smells of leather and neat's foot oil.

"*Quien es?*" asked a sleepy voice.

Gunn spoke in rapid Spanish.

"I desire to buy two horses and two saddles. I have money."

A stocky, barrel-shaped man whose skin was saddle-leather dark rose out of a pile of hay in a back corner. He blinked like a disheveled owl, wiped straw out of his black shock of hair.

"I am Juan Cardona," said the swarthy man. "I have two very fine horses to sell you. They are sound, they have the good wind and they will transport you many miles."

"Show me," Gunn said.

Juan led Gunn out back to a series of interconnected corrals. Some of the corrals contained pretty fine horseflesh.

In one corral stood five horses that Juan pointed to eagerly.

Gunn didn't like any of them.

"Is this all you have for sale?"

"Yes, These will transport you. . . ."

"I know. Many miles."

He stepped inside the corral, climbing over the rails and looked at the teeth, felt the legs, checked the chests of the five horses. Juan watched him with glittering eyes. Finally, Gunn checked the hooves. He selected two, a claybank mare and a sorrel gelding. They were both over six years old and looked to have been hard ridden. Still, they were the best of the lot.

"I'll take those two, if the price is right."

"Forty dollars each."

"I'll give you forty for the pair and I'll need some ten dollar saddles."

"Oh, the *señor* is surely joking. These are fine Mexican horses. They are easily worth fifty American dollars apiece."

"I'll give you fifty dollars for both and no more haggling."

"I will take it if you will not tell a soul how weak I am."

"Saddles and bridles," Gunn said. "Something that won't break a cinch or come apart the first time a strain is put on 'em."

After some more haggling and a lot of lying by Juan, Gunn paid for the two horses and the tack. When he was finished he had eighty dollars less in his saddlebags.

"Get the horses inside, grain 'em and curry 'em. I'll be by in the morning early."

"That will be another. . . ."

Gunn gave him four dollars so that he would not

have to listen to a long tale about how hard it was to haul in grain and water.

He stopped in at the mercantile store, bought a .31 caliber nickel-plated six-gun for Eva and a box of rimfire ammunition. The pistol could be concealed, but it would not stop anyone serious. If it made Eva feel better to have it, then it was hers. He paid six dollars for it and knew it wasn't worth over three. He hoped it wouldn't blow up in her hand.

Eva met him inside the hotel room. It was not a large room, was way in the back.

"It was all they had," she explained.

"It'll do." Gun gave her the pistol, wrapped in a piece of burlap with the box of ammunition. "Here. I got you a carpetbag too." Another sack contained a couple of dresses, an oversized purse, a carpetbag, comb, small mirror, a pair of *huaraches*.

"Oooooh!" Eva squealed, bouncing on the bed. She tried on the sandals. They fit. So did the dresses. She pranced around the room, modeling them for Gunn while he smiled with pleasure.

"I'll wash my face and then I have some nosing around to do. Hungry?"

"Starved!"

"We'll eat at the Double Eagle. Man at the mercantile said it had the best grub in town. Can you wait about an hour or so?"

"Of course! I took a bath and washed my hair. Now I can put on my dress and get some underthings. That was all you forgot."

Gunn cleared his throat.

"Well, it was hard enough getting the dresses and such."

Eva threw her arms around his neck, gave him a hearty peck on the mouth.

"You're wonderful!" she squealed.

Embarrassed, Gunn left after washing some of the dust off his face. He had strapped on a new holster and ammunition belt that he had also purchased. The holster was stiff but he rubbed some neat's foot oil inside and kneaded the leather some to make the pistol slide in and out better than it had before. The room would do for the night, he thought. A small bed, dresser, pitcher and bowl, a table, two chairs and a coat rack were the only furnishings. The mirror on the wall was cracked. The religious icons and pictures were covered with an inch of dust. The lamp was big enough to light a saloon. There were two windows and both of them had swing-out shutters that could be barred shut.

Gunn left Eva more money, told her to meet him in an hour at the Double Eagle down the street a half block. He didn't want her to wait too long before eating, but his own hunger was held in check by the task before him. It was never easy to ask questions in a strange town. From the looks of the men he'd seen outside the saloons, Tres Piedras was going to be harder than most. The population was predominantly Mexican and he stood out like a sore thumb.

The sun was just striking the face of the three rocks that rose above the plain when Gunn walked out of the hotel and turned to go into *La Copa de Oro*. The three rocks were the source of the town's name.

The cantina was quiet all of a sudden as Gunn entered.

Conversations died away. Noise stopped.

He stepped quickly aside after he came through the door. A shaft of sunlight swirled with dust motes.

His eyes took in the table, the bar.

The cantina was functional. An earth floor covered with pine needles and ground up tobacco, a crate bar, a few lamps, tables, chairs, stock on boxes and shelves.

Some of the men at the tables were old, with rheumy, vacant eyes.

Two men at the bar were younger, harder, leaner. They looked at Gunn with eyes that did not waver. Another young man sat at a table with an older man. Both were well armed. They had a bottle of *aguardiente* between them. The men standing at the bar, hips draped with mean pistols, each had a small bottle of *mezcal* from which they drank without benefit of glasses. The bartender, a large, stocky man in his early forties looked at Gunn with sleepy eyes, his hands folded across his chest. He leaned against the back wall, impervious to the flies that swarmed around him.

All of the men were Mexican.

Gunn strode to the nearest edge of the bar, three 2 x 10s nailed over sturdy pine crates.

The bartender unfolded his arms, blew a fly away from his mouth with pudgy lips. His hair was thinning, swept back straight from a bullet forehead. Gunn noticed that he wore a pistol tucked into the sash holding his apron in place. The pistol was a Sheriff's Model Colt, .36 caliber. At close range, deadly enough.

"*Señor?*"

Neither polite nor impolite. Gunn took note. The two men further down the bar both stared at him with glass beads of eyes. They wore their pistols low and each had an arm free to draw. Gunn looked straight at them as he ordered.

"Whiskey," he said.

"*Que clase?*"

"Any kind will do," Gunn said deliberately in English, "as long as it's not Forty Rod nor Taos Lightning."

"*Chit,*" said the bartender in English. "Where you think you are, greengo? In the fockin' States? We ain't got no good whiskey. It all eats out your throat and stomach. Two dollars a bottle. Fresh made." He gave Gunn a toothy grin.

"We serve only men in here," said one of the men at the far end of the bar, in Spanish. "Get the cunt a glass of milk."

Gunn understood, but gave no sign.

Instead, he fixed the bartender with a look, put his left arm on the bar. His right arm hung free. The lower part of his body was hidden behind the corner of the bar so that the two men at the other end could not see his hand. His hand floated near the butt of his Colt.

"I will have *mezcal* then," said Gunn evenly. "Bring those men at the bar glasses of milk."

"I cannot do that, *señor*. We do not have any *leche.*"

"He does not have any *leche* either," said the surly man in English, making the play on words. *Leche* in Spanish meant either milk, or sperm.

The man sounds like an expert," said Gunn to the bartender. "He has probably sucked enough of man's *leche* to know."

The talkative Mexican snapped up straight, his face

darkening with anger.

"You have insulted me, *gringo* pig!"

The Mexican went for his pistol.

Gunn slid his Colt in sight over the top of the bar.

"You move another centimeter and your hand won't work anymore," Gunn said.

"Jorge, no!" said the man standing next to the one who wanted to draw. "He will kill you!"

Jorge fumed, but remained motionless, his hand stranded in mid-air.

"Jorge Lopez meant no harm," said the bartender lamely. "He was just testing you. I am called Rosario Mendoza. Put your gun away and I will bring you some very fine *mezcal*."

"Tell Jorge down there to haul in his temper and we'll get along."

Rosario spoke rapidly to Jorge who grinned and shrugged. He turned back to the bar and picked up a drink with his gun hand. Like a rattlesnake that suddenly stops rattling, Gunn thought. The bartender brought a fresh bottle of *mezcal* and a glass. Gunn threw a cartwheel on the bar with his left hand. He holstered his pistol so that it barely rested in the leather. It would not be hard to draw if the need arose again.

Gunn poured a healthy shot of *mezcal* into the glass. Lifted it with his left hand. He nodded to the men at the end of the bar and drank slowly, never taking his eyes off Lopez.

A movement in the room caught his eye.

He did not turn his head but noted the man who had moved. Away from the table so that his feet and hands were in full view. His pistols. He wore two, high on his belt, the butts angled out from his waist. A cross-draw man.

Gunn shifted his weight to his left leg. In doing so, he half-turned so that he could see the man at the table more clearly. The man was smoking, careful to keep the smoke away from his eyes. He had a wire-thin moustache, an aquiline nose that had been broken at least twice, and big flabby ears that were framed by wide sideburns. His clothes fit him like a glove, black trousers and brown shirt. He wore a charm around his neck, a Thunderbird of silver and turquoise.

Now was probably the time to ask the question he had to ask.

The calm was only temporary, but it would have to do.

Gunn looked straight at the man sitting across from him when he spoke.

"Anybody here see a couple of wagons come through town? Last night or early this morning?"

There was an instant change in the atmosphere inside the *cantina*.

Lopez's face hardened to a bronze mask. The man next to him stiffened and gagged on his drink.

The man at the table did nothing. His eyes flickered, then glanced to the door.

Gunn heard a sound, turned slightly.

Eva stood there, pretty as anything he'd ever seen, her eyes wide, her long hair combed out, brushed to a high sheen. The sun backlit her, shone through the yellow dress she wore.

"Gunn. . . .I — —I . . . ."

Before she could say another word, Gunn heard it.

The whisper-soft sound of metal sliding out of leather.

He turned whip-fast, as Eva screamed.

SEVEN

Lopez made his move.

Gunn heard the sickening sound of the hammer snicking back.

Even as he spun into a crouch, his right hand flashing toward the butt of his Colt, he wondered if it was too late.

"Get down!" Gunn yelled to Eva.

His eyes swept the room, taking in the man at the table. The man sat still, both hands in view.

Gunn backed down in his crouch, using the bar for cover.

Lopez fired.

The bullet sizzled down the bar, struck the edge, ripping off a chunk of 2 x 10.

The Mexican fired again. The twin roars were deafening. Clouds of white smoke belched into the close air of the *cantina*.

The instant he heard the second shot, Gunn stepped out from behind the bar, still in a crouch. His Colt snug in his hand, he hammered back before he made his move.

He found his target, squeezed.

Through the haze of smoke, he saw Lopez jerk up, then totter backwards. He heard the sick splunk of the bullet as it found the Mexican's flesh, hammered into his heart muscle.

Heard the man's pistol thunk into the dirt.

The man next to him looked at Lopez in awe. Then his hands shot upward toward the ceiling.

Gunn wheeled, his pistol tracking toward the man at the table.

The man was gone!

Gunn stood up straight, glanced at the others in the room. They were frozen statues. Silent, dumb.

Eva lay sprawled on the dirt floor, her fingernails dug in.

"Anybody else?" Gunn asked. "You on the end. Get out!"

The man who had been with Lopez kept his hands high and ran, waddling, past Gunn and Eva.

Eva got to her feet. The front of her dress was soiled.

"Rosario!" Gunn barked at the bartender, "who was the man sitting in that chair over there?"

Gunn waved the barrel of his pistol toward the empty chair.

"I—I—I. . . ." the bartender stammered.

Gunn swung his pistol around to aim it at Rosario's adam's apple.

"Be quick and be certain, *amigo*," he said quietly, his gray eyes flickering with light.

"He is called Pedro Santos."

"Who is he?"

"He—he is just a man who comes in here."

"No! I want to know why he left in such a hurry. He knows something about those wagons, doesn't he?"

For emphasis, Gunn shoved the barrel a few inches closer to Rosario's face. A few inches closer to the time of the man's death.

"He knows. The wagons come through here this morning. But do not shoot me, *Señor*. Please!"

"Don't shoot him, Gunn!" shouted Eva, rushing up to him.

"I won't, if he keeps answering straight. Stay out of it, Eva!"

"I will answer you good!" insisted Rosario Mendoza. "All you has to do is ask!"

Gunn took a breath, held the pistol steady. He didn't want to let up on the pressure just yet.

"The man Santos works for. The man who is waiting for those wagons."

Rosario's face blanched. There was the un-mistakable smell of urine as he wet his pants.

"He—he will kill me if I told you!"

Gunn's face hardened.

"I will kill you if you don't, Rosario."

Eva gasped. Rosario was shaking from head to toe. His fear showed on his face. His fear gave off a scent. Tears started flowing from his eyes. The others, at the tables, looked on with pity.

"Enrico Enriquez," Gunn said. "Never heard of him."

An old man got up carefully from the table. He looked at Gunn and smiled wanly.

"You will hear much of him now," he said. "You have killed Lopez who worked for him, and Pedro Santos is his messenger. If you do not find him soon, he

73

will find you."

* * *

Pedro Santos rode up to the mouth of the canyon, out of breath.

Sunlight glinted on a rifle barrel.

Santos reined to a halt. He pulled a small hand-mirror, polished metal, flashed it at the rocks above him. He made the light bounce near where the guard sat hidden. Two longs and a short on the heliograph. The signal.

An answering signal came back.

Santos waved and rode on. Into the canyon, a half dozen miles from Tres Piedras. The walls of the canyon were blood red, as if the earth had turned to rust over the centuries.

Quail piped and in the distance he heard the boom and crackwhine of rifles. He spurred his horse, following the well-worn trail into the widening canyon.

Another guard challenged him before he got to the caves.

Santos was recognized and passed on by a grinning *cholo* wearing a machete and carrying a single-shot rifle that had seen better days.

The lean-tos were set against the sheer walls of the bluff, make-shift dwellings for those not privileged to stay out of the weather inside the natural caves. Lariats festooned with clothing hung from poles set in the earth. A spring gushed from the bluff and collected in a pool that was fenced off to keep the stock from roiling it up. Stock troughs made from halves of tarred barrels were scattered outside the perimeter and in the corrals where horses and mules nibbled on hay in the heat of the blistering sun.

Santos swung down, gave his horse to a *cholo* wearing the white uniform of the *peon*. He was a boy of twelve and unarmed.

A man standing above a group of kneeling riflemen beckoned to Santos. He took off his *sombrero*, wiped his forehead of sweat and waved that he was coming.

A row of bottles and cans were set in a line two hundred yards from the shooters.

Rifles cracked and smoke puffs scarred the air as Santos walked toward the firing line.

Ethan Morgan was helping one man load the new Sharps. His lips were parched and cracked by sun, his face as red as the cliffs that hemmed in the canyon. An armed man stood behind him, a pistol at the ready.

"Cease firing!" commanded Enrico Enriquez, as Santos hobbled up on uneven boot heels.

The shooters stood up, examined the hot rifles with admiration.

A lanky Texan looked at Santos with hooded eyes. He wore a battered Stetson, faded denims and wore a Remington .44 tied low on his leg. He had no shirt on, only a bandanna tied around his neck.

" 'Pears to me old Santos done swallowed a hair ball," drawled Jersey Slim Norris. Norris was as ruthless as he was ugly. His face looked as if it had been ripped apart and put back together by a blind god. One side was twisted where a chunk of meat had been torn out from under his cheek and the skin sewed back, pulling his eye down two notches from center, his mouth up at one corner at a 60 degree angle to his small weak chin. The Mexicans called him *"malojo"* and both feared and respected him. They thought he possessed superhuman powers. He was Enriquez' *segundo* and both men used the fear to advantage.

"What is it with you, Pedro?" asked Enriquez. "You have some bad news? It is not the soldiers again?"

Santos stopped and looked down at the *sombrero* in his hands. Then he looked up at Enriquez sheepishly.

Enriquez stood a head taller than Norris, who was taller than both Morgan and Santos. His face seemed to have been chiseled from bronze. High cheekbones jutted out over a thick beard that was horned on both sides where it jabbed at his collarbone and neck. He was all shoulder to the waist and straight down from there with lean muscular legs. He wore a knife, pistol on his belt, another pistol tucked inside, next to his hard flat belly. The khaki shirt sported epaulets. The trousers were black cord that fit tightly. His boots were Santa Fe made with fancy curlicues on the toes and tops.

"No, *mi jefe,* it is not the soldiers this time," said Santos in English. "It is a *gringo* of which much has been said along the northern trails. And he has killed Jorge Lopez as if he was a grasshopper to be squashed under his boot."

"Who is this fucking *gringo?*" asked Enriquez, more than a trace of annoyance in his deep throaty voice.

"He is called Gunn."

Morgan started to cackle with glee before the man with the pistol rammed the barrel into his kidney. Ethan winced with pain and grew silent.

"Gunn you say?" ventured Norris. His drawl was even more pronounced as he spoke through his lopsided mouth. "Name don't ding no dongs with me."

"I have never heard of such a man!" roared Enriquez, who always spoke as if he was giving a command and with the belief that the command should be carried out obediently. "How did he kill Lopez? He must have shot him in the back!"

"No, *mi jefe*, Jorge shot first. Twice. Then this Gunn shot him in the heart. It was over very fast."

"You saw this happen?" demanded Enriquez.

"I was there."

"Why did you not shoot this *gringo* then? Were you afraid of him ?"

"I was afraid of him for a very little while. He had the cold look in his eyes and it would have been no trouble for him to shoot me too. He handles the Colt *pistola* very well and he is very fast. There was a man from town having a drink with Jorge. His name is Ernesto, I think. He could not shoot either."

"You got yourself buffaloed, is all," opined Norris.

"We will hear the rest of it," ordered Enriquez, slapping Norris in the face with his curt words. "How did you get away?"

"When I saw my chance, I ran past the girl and out the door. I came here as fast as I could. This Gunn was asking about the wagons with the rifles."

At that moment, the discussion was interrupted by the squeal of women. Enriquez looked toward the encampment with annoyance.

"Those women! At it again! Someone get over there and stop that noise!"

One of the men on the firing line handed his rifle to his companion and started toward the bluffs. A scream pierced the air. Two women raced out of a cave, screeching. They were both half-naked, long hair flying.

"It's Elena Sutter, again, Jersey Slim. Take care of her."

"She's a hellcat, for shore," drawled Norris.

Elena ran her prey down, jerked her by the hair, spun her around and slashed an open palm in the girl's face. The girl screeched with pain. Some of the men around Enriquez laughed. Elena was a dusky beauty, born of a Mexican mother and a drifter named Joe Sutter. She had light hair and pale blue eyes, a straight nose and dimpled chin. She was shaped like a lamp chimney, all curves and grace, with the delicacy of blown glass in her finely chiseled features.

The other girl, a Mexican named Conchita, scratched wildly at Elena's blue eyes. Elena ducked and sent a kick into Conchita's stomach. The other girls ran out to watch and the men started drifting that way, laughing and joking among themselves. Enriquez frowned as Jersey Slim strode toward Elena. Slim was the only one who could handle her and even he was hard pressed at times to keep her in line.

Elena, like the other girls in camp, was essentially a prisoner-of-war. Booty captured in battle. Jersey had gunned down her father in a firefight on the Pecos a year ago while they were rustling cattle. Joe Sutter had the misfortune to be on the wrong side. Elena was eighteen and riding with men since she didn't like her mother. Jersey had taken her as his own prize and she had liked it for a while, but she was too wild. She wanted her freedom and if a fight broke out, nine times out of ten, Elena was at the center of it. Enriquez wished that Slim would get rid of her, but he hadn't said anything yet. Elena was a tough fighter, but she was still a woman. Women were poison, but ñecessary. Especially when they had to hide out for long periods of time. It was the only way Enriquez could prevent mutiny and assure loyalty. Let the men have their women with them, but keep them in line.

Conchita staggered back, dipped to one knee and picked up a handful of dirt to throw at Elena. Elena rushed up before she could make her move and ripped her dress down the front.

"Bitch!" Conchita exclaimed, her full breasts tumbling into view.

"Puta!" Elena slapped Conchita across the mouth, drawing blood.

But she had stepped in too close. Conchita thew out a leg, tripped Elena, then pounced on her with windmilling fists.

Elena tried to roll free. Blows rained on the top of her head. Conchita started scratching at Elena's eyes. Her hand grabbed a piece of cloth, ripped. Part of Elena's dress came away, from armpit to waist. Elena brought a knee up, smashing into one of Conchita's breasts.

Conchita fell back with a cry of pain.

Norris reached the two girls, lifted the kicking, squirming Conchita up in the air and set her down a few feet away. Elena leaped to her feet, ready to do battle. Norris stepped between the two women.

"That's about enough, ladies," he grinned, his face twisting into an even more grotesque mask.

"I'll kill her!" shouted Elena.

"Puerca!" spat Conchita.

Norris turned, kicked Conchita in the buttocks. Then he strode over to Elena, grabbed her wrist. She was covered with dirt and sweat, but his grip locked tight. He dragged her away with him as he walked back toward Enriquez and the others.

"Behave yourself or I'll pulverize you," he muttered.

Elena winced in pain, but she kept silent.

"You go ahead and finish your talk with Santos," Slim told Enriquez. "I think the trouble's over for a spell."

Enriquez shot Elena a look of controlled fury and turned back to the messenger.

"Who was the girl there?"

"Gunn called her Eva," said Santos.

"Eva! If you've harmed her. . . ." Ethan Morgan stepped toward Santos threateningly.

"Ah, you know this woman?" Enriquez turned to Morgan.

"My daughter! She was driving the other wagon. Gunn was afoot, riding with me."

Understanding flooded Enriquez's face. He scowled at Norris, then at Santos.

"Those were the two you knocked cold, Slim?"

"I reckon. We didn't see who they was. Lopez took care of one, Paco Loran dusted off the other. It was Morgan you said you wanted."

Enriquez knew a mistake had been made. There was no correcting it now. Lopez was dead, Norris had followed orders. The other man with them had been Paco Loran, who was one of the guards on duty. He could be punished.

"So, who is this Gunn, Santos? You have heard of him?"

Elena relaxed, listening. Her blue eyes glittered as she summed up the situation. She knew about the wagons and Morgan. Had heard Enriquez planning the hijacking for a long time. He wanted the rifles so that he could fight the soldiers who had pursued him for many weeks. Enrico's band of renegade misfits had stalked the Santa Fe trail from Monterey to Durango, were wanted on both sides of the border for raiding, looting, raping.

"He was the *hombre* we heard about up in the Purgatory Valley in Colorado," Santos said. "There was much talk of him. He is a killer. Do you not remember?"

"I remember something about him. Slim?"

"What the hell's he doing here?" Norris said. Elena could smell his fear-sweat. She hid her interest, but she listened intently.

"I don't know," said Enriquez, "but he is asking about the wagons, the guns. Santos, you must go into Tres Piedras and befriend this man. Tell him you know where the wagons are, then bring him here. We will be waiting."

Santos grinned.

"I will do this," he said. "Tomorrow?"

"Tomorrow. We'll have things ready by then."

Elena's eyes narrowed. There wasn't much time. She, too, had heard of Gunn. If she helped him, maybe he would help her.

EIGHT

Gunn led Eva out of the cantina.

"You could have gotten killed in there," he said, feeling her pulse race in the wrist he held. "How come you were looking for me?"

"I — I found another one of these," she said, pressing one of her father's wooden medallions in his hand.

The afternoon sun glinted in her hair. She brushed off the front of her dress as he examined the carving. It was another profile of Eva's mother, this one more finished than the first one they'd found.

"Where did you find it?"

"Wedged into a crack in that post over there. In front of the Double Eagle." Eva pointed.

Gunn walked over there, saw the crack.

"Must have stopped here, left him alone for a few minutes. We still don't know where they took your pa, but at least we know the wagons came through here."

"Gunn, I'm hungry now. Do you think I ought to change my dress?"

"No. You look fine."

"That — that man you killed in there. . . . I thought

he was going to kill you."

"So did I."

"But you knew you would kill him. You waited until the right moment. It—it was the scariest thing I've ever seen."

"Yes."

"Have you. . . .? I mean, you have killed men before, haven't you?"

Gunn nodded, sober. He handed her back the medallion, reloaded his Colt before going inside the Double Eagle.

"It must be terrible for you," she said sympathetically.

"Killing a man is hard on everyone concerned."

"It seems so final, so empty. One minute a man is alive, the next he's dead. There's nothing left. I know that man was bad. He would have killed you. But I just can't get him out of my mind. Maybe I'm worried about pa."

"Don't think about it, Eva. It won't do any good. They wanted him alive, so he's alive. We'll find him."

"I hope you're right. I hope you don't have to kill another man. Ever."

"I hope so, too, Eva." But he was not convinced.

"What will we do now?"

"Wait," he said. "They know I'm here. Someone will come looking for me."

Eva shuddered, though there was no chill. She held up her arm so that he could take it as they went inside the restaurant. His touch was warm, but she couldn't stop thinking that the hand on her arm had pulled a trigger and a man was dead.

★ ★ ★

Ethan Morgan sat under the canvas canopy looking at the array of broken rifles and pistols spread out before him. The table was an old wagon bed stretched across a pair of large flat rocks. He sat on a barrel of flour. The man who guarded him sat a few paces away, his pistol trained on Ethan's back.

His own wagon had been pulled up in front of the lean-to, so that there was some shade. Shafts of late afternoon sunlight columned through nonetheless, glittered on the barrels of the weapons. Flies buzzed, quail called from the far reaches of the canyon. Most of the Mexicans were asleep, lolling in the shade. The only voices he heard came from the women's cave. These were low and uneven sounds, punctuated by long silences as if someone in their group had shushed them when the talk became too loud.

The guard, a young intense man called 'Cadio, had been secretly nipping on cups of Maguey brought to him by his *novia*, Pilar. The Maguey was not strong, but enough of it could make a man sleepy. Ever since he had started to work, Morgan had known something was up. The wildcat, Elena, had slipped him a note. Shortly afterwards, the young girl Pilar had been bringing 'Cadio, the cool milky white drinks of Maguey. Every so often, the lad would burp noisily and then make some idiotic comment in Spanish. Morgan did not understand him, but he knew he was trying to keep anyone from finding out that he was drinking.

Ever since Ethan had arrived, he had known that his life was in jeopardy. Enriquez made it plain that he was to be another servant, instructing the men in the use of the Sharps, the proper loads, ball ammunition, some basic gunsmithing to keep them working. As well, he was expected to repair all of the misfiring, dirty and broken firearms in camp. The weapons were in a sorry state. He had the tools but not all of the parts. Still, by mixing and matching, he might be able to make most of them work again. The trouble was, Enriquez was in a hurry. There was no way he could fix the guns inside of two months. Ethan was not a hurrier.

Elena passed by out of the guard's range of vision. She made a sign to Ethan. She held up two fingers, wide apart, then closing. He understood. It would be a short while before she would be able to speak to him.

Her note had been simple:

We are going to get Lafcadio drunk. When he is asleep, I must talk to you. Elena.

Puzzled, Ethan had slipped the note in his pocket, forgotten about it. Until Pilar began sneaking up with a fresh cup of Maguey every so often, kissing 'Cadio on the mouth and neck, whispering to him.

He picked up a rusty black powder pistol. An old Colt Dragoon, .44 caliber. He slipped the hammer back to half-cock, spun the cylinder. It needed oil. At full-cock, the sear didn't engage. He tried it several times. He might be able to fix it, adapt another part to it. The Colts were good pistols, easy to fix. The man who had used it had probably used the trigger at half-cock too much, worn out the sear. Or perhaps the pistol was old and the catch had worn down smooth.

He began to take the pistol apart, glad that it was quiet. His ears still rang from the morning's shooting.

Most of the men in camp were indulging in *siestas,* but that didn't go for the lackeys, the prisoners, like himself.

He was glad Eva was alive. And Gunn. From the talk, Gunn had a reputation. Yet he had never mentioned it. It had been a mistake to think Gunn was a highwayman. But, perhaps not. Santos seemed to think he was dangerous and he had killed Lopez.

He wouldn't lose any sleep over that. Lopez had been hard on him after overpowering him and stealing the wagons. That other man, too. Paco Loran. He was like a snake. Vicious and cold.

Ethan heard a sound, half-turned, a small screwdriver in his hand.

'Cadio was trying hard to stay awake. He had leaned back and his head was tilted over his left shoulder.

Ethan turned back to the pistol, smiled to himself.

It would not be long now.

The girl, Pilar, made two more trips. Carrying cups of Maguey. 'Cadio started singing, very low, very out of tune. Then he muttered to himself. Finally, after Ethan had disassembled the pistol, laying out springs, screws, the barrel and receiver, cylinder, grips, trigger mechanism, he heard loud snoring.

Elena appeared a few moments later, dressed in men's clothing, wearing a *sombrero.* At first Ethan thought it was another guard come to relieve Lafcadio.

"Shhh!" she whispered, a slender finger over her lips.

"What is it you want?" Ethan demanded. "We could both be shot."

She knelt next to him, hunching under the table.

86

"My girlfriend and I are going to escape tonight. We want to see this man Gunn. Do you know him?"

I met him. I don't know him. Norris will kill you if you try to leave."

"Can you help us? Gunn must know who to believe. Santos is already in Tres Piedras telling this man Gunn a lot of lies. We want to warn him."

"Why are you doing this? It's dangerous. Norris or Enriquez would kill you if they knew what you were planning."

Elena's eyes flashed fire. Morgan saw the hatred there, the anger.

"Because we are prisoners here! Because Slim treats me like dirt. He is a pig. So is that greasy bastard Enriquez! I hate them!"

"All right. Calm down. I may be able to help. If my daughter Eva is with Gunn, give her this. Tell her that I am all right. Gunn must not buck this outfit by himself. I will try to do something to the guns but it might not work. Enriquez is no fool."

Ethan reached into his pocket, dug out a round piece of wood he'd been whittling on. It was another bas-relief of his dead wife.

"What is this?"

"Eva will know it's from me. That is all you will need. Good luck and Godspeed!"

Ethan watched as the girl slunk away. He sighed, went back to his work on the Dragoon. He took a small three-cornered file out of his pouch, began to work on the cocking mechanism. He doubted if the two women would make it beyond the guards. And, even so, Gunn was just one man. He stood no chance against a band of cutthroats like Enriquez's. They would cut him down without mercy.

Last night, Slim and Enrico had gloated over the rifles. Talked of their plans. They would rob those going to the fair at Taos, covering all roads with almost three dozen men. Men of the worst sort. With the new rifles, none would have a chance against them. He tried to think of a way to thwart the Mexican bandit's plans. Perhaps a last minute inspection of the the new rifles would give him a chance to jam them.

How could he do that? He would be watched like a hawk. One false move and they'd gun him down. Still, there had to be a way, if he could only think of one.

Ernesto Cornejo looked at his hands.

They had finally stopped shaking. The moths in his belly had stopped fluttering. But the fear was still there, snugged up against his spine, spidery claws holding on to a nerve end. The fear was dormant, but he knew it was there. Threatening his manhood. Pulling him into a cowardly slump whenever he thought about the *gringo* who had shot down Lopez as if swatting a fly. Faster than any man he'd ever seen. Fast and deadly. And he could have shot both of them. Easy. He had never seen anything like it in his life. One minute Lopez was alive, breathing and shooting. The next, his back was flying apart, his heart shot to a bloody pulp.

"You keep looking at the door to the Double Eagle," said his companion, Pepe Barrios. "Is there someone you are meeting there in a little while?"

"Yes," said Ernesto tightly. "I am going to kill someone pretty soon."

Pepe looked through the grime-caked pane in the El Saguaro across the street. The sun threw long shadows down the street which ran east and west. He felt a shiver of cold. The bottle of *mezcal* was nearly empty, but it was only a pint. Ernesto had not drunk much since he had stopped shaking.

"I just sat down to talk a minute about Lopez," said Pepe, hoping to change the subject. Lopez was on everyone's mind, his name on the lips of those who told versions of the shooting. Pepe had gotten the news only a short while before and knew only that Lopez had been shot by a stranger, a *gringo* and that his friend Ernesto had been having a drink with the bandit when it happened. "I was wondering who the stranger was and why he killed Lopez? Were they enemies, then?"

"It was a very fast thing," said Ernesto, staring out the window, trying to push down the fear crawling back up his spine. "I do not think that Lopez ever saw the stranger before. But he made me leave the cantina like a whipped dog and I do not like that very much."

"Pepe had heard that Ernesto threw his hands in surrender and then ran away. But he would not mention this to his friend. It was an ugly thing that one did not talk about in public. There was no honor in such behavior. It stank of cowardice and unmanliness.

"This man, he is very *macho*, no?"

Ernesto's cheeks flared red. His eyes drew down to oval cracks. He picked up his glass furiously and tossed down the *mezcal*. It did not seem to affect him at all.

"He is a *gringo* swine!" blurted Ernesto. "I was caught by surprise. There was much noise and much smoke. I thought he was going to shoot me down and I did not have a quarrel with the man. I did not draw my gun nor insult him. I was merely drinking with Lopez. He had the pistol aimed at me, Pepe, and he was very fast. He had a way to hit the hammer and make the pistol ready for shooting very fast. I think he is a gunfighter."

This is what Pepe wanted to hear. The small details.

"Lopez was very fast, too. He was most dangerous with the pistol and the knife."

"Clearly. But this *gringo* was much faster."

"I have heard that he is called Gunn. That he is from the north and has killed many men."

Ernesto's eyebrows went up, shaping into quizzical arches.

"You have heard talk of this man?"

"Only a little. They say that he fought the Apaches, that he shot Cartucho."

Ernesto felt the fear climb a little higher up his spine. He drew his pistol impulsively and half-cocked it, spun the cylinder. There were six bullets in the converted Remington. They were good bullets. The pistol was oiled. He hoped it would not misfire.

"Was he the one who was up on the *Purgatorio?*"

"They say he is the same, Ernesto."

"Jesus Christ!"

"He is one mean *hombre,* I think."

"Mother of God."

"You should not swear so much, Ernesto."

"I hate that bastard. He made a fool of me."

"You are alive. He could have killed you."

"Maybe that would have been better. I do not want to be remembered as a coward."

"Who will remember you if you are dead? You have

no family."

"I have a family!" Ernesto snapped. For a moment Pepe thought his friend was going to shoot him. It was not good to be around an angry man, especially one so angry as Ernesto. Pepe shrank back in his chair, bowed his head meekly. His battered hat shaded his face. The sun turned the liquid in his glass to amber. It was very quiet in the cantina. Most of the drinkers were at the Copa, the scene of violence a short time before. The bartender in El Saguaro was asleep, snoring softly, an undertone to the lazy buzzing of flies.

Ernesto made a sound in his throat, looked out the window again. His family was in Guerrero, many kilometers from Tres Piedras. He had a wife, children. He wondered if he would ever see them again. They were very poor, lived in the remote mountains. He sent them money every so often but they never replied. None of them knew how to write and he could only write a few words himself. It was not important. He meant to go back someday, but he didn't want to be poor. That was why he had made friends with Lopez. He wanted to ride with Enriquez and Lopez had said that might be possible. Now, he wondered. He did not know Enriquez, only his reputation.

Ernesto had dreams and they had been soiled by the *gringo* stranger.

The sun glazed the pane, burnished it to a gold orange. For a moment, Ernesto was blinded.

The door to the Double Eagle opened and he saw a woman's figure. At first he thought it was another splash of sun, but the windows on the opposite side of the street were dark with shadows. Eva's yellow dress brightened as she stepped into the street. Behind her, two paces, came Gunn, his face struck with light on one side, the other side bathed in shadow.

Pepe saw the look in Ernesto's eyes, peered through the pane.

He gulped deeply, scraped his chair.

"That is the man?" he asked softly.

"He is the one I am going to kill."

Ernesto saw the girl stop, wait for Gunn. They were on the far side of the street. There was time to walk to the door and step outside, challenge the *gringo* in front of everyone. Gunn would have the sun in his favor, but that couldn't be helped. The Mexican stood up, holstered his pistol, pulled his hat brim down over his eyes for shade. He knocked over his glass, startling Pepe.

Ernesto steeled himself, went to the door. The two were still there in the street, laughing. The woman had her arm linked in Gunn's left arm. It would be too bad if she was in the way. He stepped outside, stood a pace away from the open door of the *cantina*.

"You there!" he called in English. "Gunn! I am going to shoot you dead!"

Gunn looked up.

Ernesto felt the pale gray eyes bore into his chest.

The fear clambered up his spine, a bristly beast with sharp rattling claws.

NINE

Gunn saw the Mexican standing just outside El Saguaro, his legs close together, his right hand hovering over the butt of his pistol.

It took him a second or two to place the man.

"Eva," he said under his breath, "when I push you, fall down and stay down."

Eva's fingers dug into his arm. She looked up at Ernesto, her face white with fear.

"You hear me, *gringo?*"

Gunn detected the slight slur. The man had drink in him. The sunlight glanced off of bead-brown eyes, bronze skin shot with vermillion on the cheekbones.

"I have no quarrel with you," Gunn said, his voice carrying across the street.

"You have shamed me, man."

"It was not your fight, mister. It's over. All over. Go back inside the cantina. Have yourself a drink. Tomorrow will look better to you."

Faces appeared in windows. People came out of the hotel, the Copa de Oro. They stayed close to the protection of the walls, the adobe. Curious, they watched the man in the street, standing with the girl in the yellow dress. They whispered who he was and smelled the aroma of burning powder although no shots had been fired. The word passed up and down the street that Gunn was about to shoot someone. Again. The whispers carried weight. The weight of promise and of fear.

"I want satisfaction," Ernesto blurted in Spanish. "I am going to shoot you down."

Gunn's right hand inched toward his pistol butt. The hand moved slow as if wading through deep fast waters. The movement was almost imperceptible. There was a showdown here and he didn't know how to get out of it. The Mexican was liquored up and his manhood was bruised. Gunn had seen it before, usually in the very young. A name was called, an insult given, and suddenly the bright face of honor was tarnished. It was a terrible thing to die for, a senseless thing. It made him very sad.

"I do not know your name," Gunn said. "If I've offended you, I am sorry. I did not want to shoot the other man. He pushed it. You know that, don't you?"

"I know that. He is not my concern now. You took advantage of me. I do not want to live with that shadow over me."

Eva tensed, dug deeper into Gunn's arm.

"Steady," he said, under his breath. "The man is *loco*. He's liable to go off at any time."

"Gunn, I'm scared. Plumb scared."

"You go down, eat some dirt when I tell you."

Ernesto stepped forward another pace. This time, his legs spread wide in an aggressive stance.

"No more talk, man!" His hand dropped closer to

the butt of his pistol. "I am calling you out, Gunn! You fucker!"

Gunn let it pass. He wasn't going to be goaded into a fight if he could avoid it. His eyes moved quickly. Saw the gathering gawkers. He cursed under his breath. They wanted a show. The Mexican would notice it too and go for it because he was proud.

"Your name?" Gunn asked again.

"I am called Ernesto. Ernesto Cornejo from Guerrero."

"Ernesto, don't push this. Let's have a drink together and talk it all out."

Gunn watched the man's face. The sun shaped it into a bronze sculpture, chiseled out all the shadows, left the lean sharp edges. The eyes were wild, squinted now as the sun dropped lower, bathed the side of the street in light. He saw the bloodlines of the savage, tempered with the ferocity of the Moors, forged in the Latin cauldron of Spanish earth. He saw the puma and the wolf, the dove and the hawk. He saw the pain and the pride, the fear and the anger of centuries. He saw a man willing to die for principles he didn't understand, but were part of his blood and his heart. He saw a soldier in the front line, his flag shot to ribbons, no longer waving in the blood scented breeze of battle. Ernesto was standing on the final ground, the *querencia* of the bullring, not the matador, but the bull itself, shoulders crimson, the tendons weakened by the *banderillas*.

Gunn stood there with the killing sword close at hand.

"I am a man!" shouted Ernesto.

And went for his gun.

Eva screamed as Gunn shoved her hard. She fell to one side, sprawling in the dirt of the street.

Breaths sucked in. Eyes darted to Gunn.

He crouched. His hand flew like the shadow of a deep-swimming fish toward the butt of his pistol.

The scene played out in slow motion.

With an anguished cry, Ernesto grasped the butt of his pistol, drew faster than he had ever drawn before.

His jaw set hard as his teeth ground together in fierce determination. He was fast and he knew it.

But Gunn was faster.

His pistol came to hand, cocked, bucked twice. Blew hot lead toward Ernesto's gut. He shot low, feeling the bullets hit, raising the pistol for the killing shot to the head if it became necessary. The shot he hoped he didn't have to squeeze off.

Dust puffed up from Ernesto's shirt. Blood spread out in a crimson stain just above his belt buckle.

He pulled the trigger of his pistol knowing the barrel wasn't high enough. Dust kicked up in front of Gunn's boots.

The pistol weighed a long ton and he felt the shock and the pain. The blood surged up in his ears, became a roaring sound that was like water crashing through a narrow canyon carrying boulders along in a flood rush of excitement and danger. The sound thinned to the tintinnabulation of far off trumpets. He heard the dark hoofbeats of cavalry racing across an empty plain and the flap of banners.

He saw Gunn standing there with a smoking pistol in his hand.

Ernesto saw the enemy and tasted the coppery rinse of defeat on his lips.

He staggered forward, summoning up reserve of pride-born strength. He brought the heavy pistol up for a killing shot.

Gunn stood there, frozen, his gun arm high, his pistol held straight out. A statue holding firm, splashed by the red-orange rays of the sun.

On the ground, Eva looking at him, her face white, her long hair draped over her shoulders. Her lips quivering, tongue flicking over them like a cat's.

He started to squeeze the trigger and time stopped.

Smoke blossomed from the black hole of Gunn's pistol barrel.

Sparks and flame speared through the smoke.

Ernesto kept squeezing the trigger, but there was no feeling in his finger. The pistol did not jump in his hand. There was only the longest of silences and then a crack as if someone had snapped a guitar string. The music sounded a single eerie note and the blood behind his eyes turned to ink.

Gunn saw the hole appear in Ernesto's forehead. The back of his skull flew apart, blood spraying in a 180 degree arc of pink. Brain and bone chunks splattered on the wall behind the Mexican, smeared slime on the window where Pepe's face hung like a child's balloon, all eyes and mouth and transfixation.

Ernesto's legs went out from under him. He fell backwards, slumped in a grotesque heap.

"You killed him," Eva breathed.

Gunn lowered his pistol. His shoulders sagged.

"Yes, dammit, I killed him."

Gunn thumbed the hammer back, spun the cylinder of his Colt. He lined up the empty hulls, worked the ejector rod. The brass slid free, thunked to the street.

He rammed in fresh bullets, jammed the Colt back in its new holster. He looked around belligerently at the townspeople as Eva got to her feet.

"Somebody here know this man?" Gunn shouted.

Pepe came to the door of the saloon, *sombrero* in his hand. He kneaded the brim with nervous fingers, nodded.

"He was my friend," said the Mexican.

Gunn reached in his pocket, fished out a twenty dollar gold piece. He flipped it to Pepe.

"See that he gets buried proper."

To the rest of the gawking townsfolk Gunn had more to say.

"Get on back to your stores and houses," he ordered. "And tell your kids that this man didn't die with honor. He died stupid."

Some people gasped. Gunn snorted, turned to Eva, a look of disgust etched in his face. She cringed at the look she saw in his eyes.

"I—I'm sorry, Gunn," she said. "Truly sorry. I know you tried to stop that man."

"Let's go," he said gruffly, jerking her arm. He stalked to the hotel, Eva in tow, past a clump of men waddling up to help Pepe with Ernesto's body. Others cleared a path for him, shrinking out of his way.

In their room, Gunn began peeling out of his shirt. He poured water into a bowl, set the pitcher down with a ringing thud of porcelain. He scrubbed his hands, dried them with a fresh towel. Eva sat on the edge of a chair, watching him.

"You feel dirty, don't you?" she said. Her voice was weak, quavery.

He fixed her with a sharp look, threw the towel

down next to the pitcher and bowl.

"Dirty enough. That was bad business. Senseless."

"You can't blame yourself for what happened."

"I don't. I blame no one. Least of all Ernesto Cornejo. He did what he felt he had to do. It was just wrong, that's all. He wasn't a gunfighter. He wasn't even much of a man."

Eva rose from the edge of her chair, came to Gunn. There was a faint glittering light in her eyes.

Gunn had seen that look before.

A fascination for death. For danger. It was a natural thing, but it always bothered him. Death was not fascinating to the one who did the killing. It was ugly. A reminder of the beast inside every man, every woman.

"You've killed twice today. Two men. How do you feel afterwards? What goes through your mind when you shoot and know your bullet is going to kill someone?"

"Jesus, Eva."

"Please. I want to know. I watched you out there." She shuddered. "Like ice. I thought you were going to let him shoot you. That's the same way I felt the other time, when Lopez was shooting at you. I was screaming inside. Shoot him! Kill him, Gunn! But I couldn't say anything. I could only watch and wonder what you were thinking. It must have been awful."

There is a moment just before you pull the trigger when you wonder if you can pull it and shoot a man dead. Then, there is an explosion. The explosion is in the mind first, then in the hand and it's too late to think, to look back and that awesome moment comes when the earth opens up and you feel yourself falling into a crevice where there is only darkness and a long sadness. And the chasm is a grave and you're falling into your own grave and all that's left is for someone to throw dirt on top of you and cover the mound with stones and say some words and forget you were ever there. It was hell to kill a man. It was hell to go on living after you did. but some men needed killing and they seemed to want to die with that explosion going off, with the roar of black powder igniting and flame pushing a ball of lead through the air faster than the eye could see. Death, violent death, held an appeal for such men but it was still no good. Not for the man still standing up, a smoking pistol in his hand, the sound of the explosion still ringing in his ears like the tail end of a terrible symphony heard in an empty music hall.

"Gunn? Are you going to answer me?" She looked up at him, saw the vacant stare in his cold pewter eyes.

"Huh? There is no answer, Eva. You called it right."

She put her arms around his waist, flattened her cheek to his bare chest. He felt her trembling.

"Hold me," she said. "Hold me tight. I—I'm scared."

"Of me?"

"Of everything. It was awful, wasn't it?"

"Yes."

He hugged her tight to him, felt the warmth of her body.

"I need you," she said. "Need you bad, Gunn."

She moved her arms up to his neck, pulled herself up so that their faces were close. Their lips moved together, touched. Fire seeped through their flesh.

Eva was still trembling.

Gunn knew how it was with her. She felt mortal

after witnessing death at close hand. She was in a kind of shock—a shock that had jolted her senses so that she needed proof of being alive. Proof that she was a woman fullblown, capable of reproducing, continuing the strain of human beings from whose loins she had sprung. He had seen such reactions before when men and women had coupled in the midst of a fierce Indian attack, or when a natural disaster had threatened them. It was an act of survival, borne of some deep instinct to preserve the human race even though one or both might die.

"Come," he husked, "I'll take you to bed."

Her face lit up with an eager shining. Quickly, she squirmed out of her dress, bared her sleek skin.

The afternoon light glowed on the shades in the room.

Gunn stripped naked, carried her to the bed. Her trembling had given way to an eager quivering. They lay together atop the covers, embraced.

Her hand found his manhood, squeezed the growing stalk gently.

"This is what I want," she whispered.

"It's yours, Eva."

He grew bone hard as she stroked him. He played with her breasts, kissed her hungry mouth. His hand roamed her naked body, slid down to the thatched crevice between her thighs. In silence they explored each other with touches, kissing as the pressure built between them, as the glowfire in their loins grew in intensity.

"I'm hot, Gunn. So hot I can't stand it."

It was time. He rolled her on her back, rose above her. She spread her legs to receive him and he saw the pink folds of flesh beneath the furred triangle. He sank into her, feeling her spasm as the crown of his organ passed through the open portal of her sex. He sank into bubbling lava, his spine tingling from the electric surge through his loins.

It was sweet, the sinking.

"Oh!" she exclaimed, her body bucking with a sudden orgasm.

He held her tight around the shoulders, sank deeper through the steaming folds of flesh. The sweetness grew. He pumped her slow, exulting in each stroke. The pressure, the warmth, the wetness. The mystery, at once opening and deepening. Her eyes danced with light. Her body shimmered sleek in the wan orange light of afternoon. The bed creaked like a summer porch swing, lazy, comforting. Her soft breathing, shallow and quick, was like faintly heard music. The feel of her flesh against his legs, his belly, his chest, was another part of the pleasure.

He forgot about Cornejo.

There was only Eva now. She thrashed again, her fingers burying their tips in his arms. He felt the intensity of her orgasm and that, too, gave him pleasure. He stroked her slow, keen to her desires, her needs. She began to move with him, pushing upward to bury his shaft deep in her cleft, deep in her love-tunnel. She matched his movements and they pleasured in the slow rhythms, the sudden spasms, the unexpected eruptions as she climaxed again and again. The room darkened gradually, closing them in to each other, smothering them in tawn shadow.

"Let me have your seed," she said, finally, panting from the sudden rush of orgasmic pleasure.

"I can stay longer,"

"I know. I want you to be happy too." There was a sad lilt to her voice as if she knew it would end and couldn't bear it any longer.

"I am happy."

"Me too. But I want you to feel what I'm feeling right now."

He knew what she meant. Pleasure shared was pleasure doubled. Just as sadness shared was sadness halved.

He grasped her to him, increased the speed of his stroking. She bucked with shattering orgasms, exciting him until he felt the boil and rush of his seed. He rocketed up as his seed burst from the sac, spewed into the mouth of her womb. He shuddered with pleasure. She dug her fingers into his arms, slid her hands around to his back.

"Oh, yes!" she screamed softly. "Yes, Gunn, yes!"

Their bodies twitched in final spasms, stilled.

The room was silent except for the sound of their breathing.

He rolled away from her, exhausted, filled.

The moments stretched into eternities as they lay side by side with their thoughts.

"Gunn," she said finally, "do you know what 'unrequited love' means?"

"No. That's a four-bit word. I don't know many of them."

"I heard it from my mother once. She was trying to tell me about a boy she was sweet on when she was a girl. He never even noticed her and it broke her heart. 'Unrequited' means that you don't give love back when you want it. You love someone and they don't even know it. It hurts bad. But I guess I can accept it."

"I don't know what you mean," he said feeling uncomfortable.

"I mean I love you, Gunn. And I know you don't love me. Not the same way."

There was nothing he could say. Eva was right. And it hurt. It hurt both of them.

He wanted a cigarette. He wanted to sleep. He wanted a hole he could crawl into and be alone with the thoughts that kept crowding in on him.

He kept seeing Cornejo's face again in those last moments of his life. Only now, Cornejo was grinning, laughing at him.

He closed his eyes and the image went away.

Laurie's face appeared in his mind. Then Eva's.

"I love you, Gunn," Eva said again, quietly. Her voice was far away. "I love you even if you don't love me. Even if. . . ."

He knew what she was going to say.

"Even if you *can't* love me."

"I'm grateful," he said.

A squeeze on his arm. He didn't open his eyes.

"Thank you for that," she whispered.

Her sobbing wrenched at him and when he opened his eyes, it was dark in the room and he was more alone than he had been in a long time.

TEN

Pedro Santos looked at the waxen face of Ernesto Cornejo.

The eyes were closed, the flesh sagging away from the dark circles around the eyes. The black hole in his forehead was neat, blue-black around the edges. They had laid him out and washed away most of the blood. They had put silver dollars over the eyes to keep them closed until the flesh stiffened. A woman in black sat in a corner of the room, muttering her beads. A candle burned, the aroma mixing with the death smell. Someone had put flowers in the room, tied a pale yellow ribbon around the can full of dirt.

Pepe was sniffling, hawking phlegm.

"We brought him here because he does not have family."

"You should bury him right away before he ripens," said Santos.

"Some men are digging a grave," slobbered Pepe. "*Dios mio*, it was so fast. Ernesto he didn't have no chance."

"Ernesto was stupid. Where is that *cabron* Gunn

now? Drinking his victory?"

Santos had ridden into Tres Piedras only moments before, heard about the shooting. Someone had directed him to Pepe's adobe shack on one of the back streets. A huddle of women and children outside had told him which adobe was Pepe's. Women made a great deal over death. Children were fascinated by its mystery. It was a stupid thing. Cornejo wasn't there anymore. Neither was his spirit. All that was left was an empty carcass stripped of life. When the breath went, the soul went. To God knows where. It didn't matter. A man dead was not a man anymore. That was what made his belly tighten as it was now.

"He went to the hotel with that *gringa,*" said Pepe, wiping a sleeve under his dripping nose. "Ernesto was very brave, *Señor* Santos. He was pretty fast, too."

"Not fast enough, eh?"

Santos looked at the hole in the shirt near Cornejo's belly button. The cloth was still wet, but the blood hadn't washed out. He saw a piece of white flesh underneath. Gruesome, sickening. The attempt at bravado didn't help. Gunn wasn't going to be easy. He would have to be very careful. Now might not be a good time to try and meet the man, take him into his confidence. Tomorrow would be better, after the man had slept and rested.

"Did this man Gunn use any tricks, Pepe?"

"No. He tried to talk Ernesto out of the fight. I watched the whole thing from the window in the cantina. I could hear every word. I thought the *gringo* was a coward at first. He did not want to fight."

"But Cornejo pushed it, did he?"

"He was very angry at that man. He wanted to kill him."

Santos snorted. He turned away from the dead man.

The woman in the corner stopped muttering and looked up at him. Saw that his hat was still on his head. She pointed a gnarled crooked finger at him accusingly.

"Cross yourself," she said through cracked teeth, "and have the decency to remove your hat. The Holy Ghost is here. The spirit of the Lord is watching over this poor dead man."

Santos took off his hat. He did not make the sign of the cross.

"Pray for him, Mother," he said, shrugging a gesture for Pepe to go outside. "Pray for us all."

The old crone snorted and went back to her rosary. The muttering descended into a low keening chant of satisfaction. The candle flickered, shaking up the shadows in the room. For a moment, Santos thought Cornejo's eyes had opened. It was only a trick of the light, but it was unnerving.

Santos crossed himself quickly, surreptitiously.

The old woman looked up and flashed a gap-toothed smile.

Outside, in the gathering dark, Santos walked up to the waiting Pepe. He grabbed the man's elbow, shoved him out of earshot of the adobe's mourners still huddled near the door as if conducting a vigil for a man who might come back to life at any time and appear in their midst.

"Pepe, do you want to make a little money?" Santos asked, his voice dropped to a conspiratorial whisper. He snugged his hat back on his head, looked back into the *jacal* where the people begn to squat down like roosting chickens.

"I am not sure."

"This will be easy money."

"No money is easy."

"To the point, *amigo*, this is easy money. All you have to do is one or two simple little things."

"What simple little things?"

"First, you will go to the hotel and make sure that this Gunn is there and that he is not going to leave tonight. That is simple, no?"

"Maybe," Pepe shrugged. "And what is the other thing?"

"In the morning, you will talk to this man and tell him what I will tell you."

"He will maybe shoot me?"

"No. He will be glad to hear what you have to say." Santos was being very patient with Pepe. He needed him, but he would have to treat him like a child. Pepe was a man who lived for the next drink and seldom had the price to pay for one.

"How much will you pay for these little things?" Pepe asked.

"I will give you five dollars."

Pepe cocked his head, considering the offer. His eyes narrowed cannily. Santos fixed him with a frosty smile.

"It is not much money. Perhaps this *gringo* will not like what I tell him."

"You want more money? I will give you ten dollars. That will buy you much *mezcal*, Pepe."

Pepe licked his lips. Santos had made a strong point. Ten dollars would buy a lot of *mezcal*.

"You are going to shoot this Gunn?"

Santos laughed; a dry, harsh laugh that stirred the

squatters in the *jacal*.

Pepe shivered and looked up at the dark sky over the adobe. The stars had begun to wink and the bats were feeding, knifing through the air on silent wings, emitting piercing squeaks that sounded like terrorized mice.

"No, Pepe. I am going to be friends with him."

Santos reached in his pocket, separated some bills. He held up two fives. He gave one to Pepe.

"This is for me?"

"Five now, and another five when you have delivered the message to Gunn."

Pepe took the bill, swallowing quickly. He buried it in his fist as if to discourage Santos from taking it back.

"Tell me what you want me to say to this Gunn," he said.

Santos threw an arm around Pepe's shoulder.

"Listen, Pepe. Tell him these things exactly. . . ."

★   ★   ★

Paco Loran stood in the center of the cave, cringing.

"Next time I give you a job to do, maybe you'll do it right!" snapped Enriquez. He paced back and forth, cracking a three-stranded quirt for emphasis. The short whip held Paco's gaze. Every time it cracked, he jumped. "You let a bastard get away that's causing me all kinds of trouble. Lopez is dead! The gunsmith had a daughter with him. What the hell went on in your stupid brain?"

"*Patron,*" whimpered Paco, "I followed your orders.

You said to capture Morgan and bring him to you along with the wagons and the rifles. Lopez, he did not kill this man either. We did not know there was a girl."

Enriquez turned savagely and lashed out with the quirt. The leather thongs whipped across Paco's face, striping it with crimson streaks. Paco cried out, then bit his lip until the blood oozed.

"Excuses! Get out of here, Paco, and don't let me see your face for twenty-four hours. Or I might kill you!"

Paco needed no urging to leave the cave. He was glad that the others hadn't seen what the *patron* had done to him. His fingers touched the welts on his face. They stung more than his flesh. His pride had been hurt. Enriquez had done this thing to others and it had been a laughing matter among the men. Now, it was different. He had to redeem himself with the *patron*. He was no fool, but had only followed the orders of Lopez. He had not known that Gunn was there, nor the girl. Two shapes in the night, under blankets. He had thought they were *peones,* workers hired by the gunsmith, Morgan. Lopez hadn't told him to kill anyone. It was a mistake, but Enriquez would not listen to reason. He was angry and his wrath was a terrible thing to see.

Paco slunk along the side of the bluff, afraid to show his face even in the dark. He did not want anyone to see the marks of the whip on his face. He headed toward the lean-to where the women stayed. Perhaps Junia could give him some Maguey. He reached down, grabbed a handful of dirt and rubbed it over his face. The dirt would hide the welts. He could say that he had fallen and scratched his face on the mesquite.

He had known what was coming when his relief

came. Enriquez had wanted to see him, alone. He had already heard about Santos going into town to try and lure the *gringo* to the encampment. He could have done a better job than Santos, but *el patron* no longer trusted him. That was a hurt too, worse than the whip-streaks across the face. Lopez had been number one, after Jersey Slim. Then, he and Santos were on equal footing. And now Lopez was dead. But he was back to the bottom of the pile.

At first Paco's hatred was an indefinable thing. It wavered from one object to another, like a moth seeking a flame. At first, he hated Lopez for fucking the monkey. And then, Enriquez for not listening to reason. And now, as he walked along the wall of the bluff, he hated Morgan, the *gringo,* for being the original cause. He had said nothing about his daughter. Nothing about the gunfighter they called Gunn. Nothing. The bastard. The son of bad milk.

Paco stopped in front of the lean-to where the guns were laid out on tables, sticking out of boxes.

"*Oye,* Morgan," he slurred. "Come out here, *cabron* and let my fists find your stupid face."

He called in a loud whisper toward the tent where he knew the gunsmith was sleeping.

A Mexican he knew appeared out of the shadows. A man named Cardenas. Miguel, he thought.

"Hey, *chico,* you make a lot of noise," said Cardenas. "You want me to blow your fucking face off?"

"I am looking for the stupid *riflero,* Cardenas. I want to break his goddamned neck."

"It's you who will have the broken neck and probably get your balls cut off and stuffed up your ass

111

if you don't get out of here. This Morgan is important to the *patron* and I will see to it that he sleeps like a babe without worrying about *basura* like you."

Paco growled low in his throat, but he saw the movement of the rifle barrel. A shadow shape that disappeared. He knew the barrel was pointed at his head. A second later he heard the snick of the action as Cardenas put the hammer on full cock.

"Chit, man," said Paco in English. "I was only trying to have some fun. I would not hurt the *gringo*. After all, it was I who captured him, no?"

Cardenas laughed. But he did not move the rifle barrel. Instead, he stepped back a pace and lost himself in shadow. His laughter died away.

"Move on. Go get yourself a woman and some *licor*. The sun must have baked your fucking brains, *amigo*."

"Ay, clear. True. The truest of true. I will see Junia and put my mouth on her tit and see if she responds."

"You'll shit in a barrel," cracked Cardenas, moving back toward Morgan's tent.

Paco backed off, angered now at Cardenas. Killing Morgan would have given him satisfaction. But of course Cardenas was right. Enriquez wanted him alive. For a time. Maybe, after the twenty-four hours was up he would ask the *patron* if he could be the one to kill Morgan. That might prove that his heart was strong and that he could serve well.

Paco shuffled past the post holding up the canvas lean-to over the work tables. Toward the cave where the women stayed. He hoped he did not run into Jersey Slim. That was a man he genuinely feared.

It was dark as pitch in the canyon, but Paco knew it

by heart.

Before he reached the cave, he heard soft whispers. Not the usual laughing. It brought him up short.

Something was not quite right.

He stopped in the shadow of a water barrel, listening.

Girls' voices drifted to him. He couldn't make out the words. The girls were whispering and that piqued Paco's curiosity. He hunched closer to the barrel, hugging it so that the two shadows were one. From the sound of the voices, the girls were coming closer.

"Did you get the horses?" he heard one of them whisper. He recognized the voice.

Elena Sutter!

"Shh! They're picketed a little ways from the corral."

The other voice too, he knew.

Junia Diaz passed within four feet of Paco's hiding place.

The two girls were dressed in dark clothing, carried bundles under their arms. He couldn't see their faces, but could tell who they were by their size and shape. Both wore straw hats that made rustling noises as the brims brushed together. Junia was leading Elena away from him now, toward the corral where the horses were kept.

"Do you think we can make it?" asked Elena.

"If we're careful. The wrangler is asleep."

"Drunk, you mean."

Paco heard Junia giggle and his senses jangled as he realized what the girls were up to.

They were going to escape!

Paco held his breath, waiting for them to pass out of

113

earshot. The information was valuable. He could redeem himself in Enriquez's eyes. But what should he do? Grab them and sound the alarm? Or follow them, see what they were up to? Jersey Slim would be very angry if Elena ran away. He'd probably kill her if he caught her trying to do such a thing.

The girls stooped and crept in a widening pattern away from the caves until he lost sight of their silhouettes.

His own horse was picketed at a grassy spot on the other side of the canyon valley. It would not take him long to saddle up and follow the girls. He might be able to learn more if he followed them. If he caught them now, they would only lie and might involve him.

Paco made his decision.

★   ★   ★

Pepe Barrios rubbed his eyes, blinked them.

He was trying hard to stay awake. He had slept some, but not enough. Twice he had gone to the door, put his ear against it. He had heard the breathing inside the room. Isolated two separate distinct patterns of breathing. The two sleepers were still inside. The girl and the man they called Gunn.

He squatted in a far corner of the hall, waiting for his man to emerge. That could be at dawn, or after the sun was up. There was no way of telling. Pepe told himself that if the man did not come out after the sun was up, he would knock on the door and deliver the message. He wanted that other five dollars from Santos. His thirst now was a powerful thing, aggravated by loss of sleep. He knew a cantina that would open soon

114

and he could already taste the raw scratch of *mezcal* in his throat.

Pepe licked his lips, stood up. One of his feet was starting to go numb. He wiggled his toes inside his boot to restore circulation. The toes began to tingle.

Spines of feeling ran up his leg. He paced on tiptoes trying to regain the feeling in his extremities. A board creaked underfoot. Pepe froze at the sound, amplified in the narrow hallway. He listened but no one opened a door to challenge him. He turned, went back to his corner. This time, he stood up as feeling flowed back into his toes. He leaned against the wall and closed his eyes. Just for a minute.

Gunn awoke with a start.

His hand reached out instinctively for the pistol hanging on the bedpost. His hand slid over the butt. He jerked it from the leather.

Someone was moving out in the hall.

He heard a board creak.

Twice before he had partially roused, startled by something. A faint sound. The scrape of a sole on wood. But no one had tried to break in so he had gone back to sleep. A shallow sleep that was like being in a stupor. Now, he looked around the room. It was so pitch black that he could make out only a few familiar objects. He looked at Eva asleep next to him. Sensed more than saw her. Her shape on the bed, curled up, naked, only a thin sheet covering her, a whiteness like snow.

But someone was outside.

He heard the pressure of a body striking the wall. A slight sound but it carried and was like the creak of an old house at midnight.

Gunn slipped out of bed, sought his trousers in the dark. He laid the pistol on the bed where he had lain. He put on his pants, his shirt and socks. He did not put on his boots. He strapped on his gunbelt, slid the pistol back in its holster.

Quietly, he walked to the door.

He lifted the latch, moving it a fraction of an inch at a time.

He made no sound.

The door opened wide enough for him to slip through.

He peered into the hall.

There was more light there. A glow arose from the stairs, but there were no lamps lit on the second floor. All of the doors he could see were closed. He stuck his head further into the hall.

A jellied chill moved through his veins.

A man stood in the corner, leaning against the two walls.

Gunn quelled the fear that rose up involuntarily.

Something was odd about the figure.

Gunn waved a hand in front of his own face. The figure didn't move. Then it dawned on him that the man was asleep!

He stepped out in the hallway, drew his pistol. He started toward the man, the pistol uncocked. His feet made only a faint whispering sound on the board flooring.

He walked right up to the man, stuck the pistol out at arm's length two feet from the man's face.

Hammered back.

Pepe Barrios jumped, a cry rising up his throat, stillborn.

"Make no sound, *amigo*," Gunn said softly. "Or you'll end up papering the wall."

"Jesus the Christ," Pepe said in Spanish, a guttural whisper.

"Keep your hands up where I can see 'em," ordered Gunn. "And tell me real careful and slow what the hell you're doing skulking around out here."

Pepe gulped. His eyes went wide with fear.

"I mean you no harm," he said in English. "I have the message for you. It is from a friend. He wants to be your friend."

Warily, Gunn eyed the trembling man.

"Let's have it, then," he said.

"His name is Santos. You know him, I think. He said to tell you he was the one in the *cantina* when you killed Lopez."

"A gunny. I saw him. What about it?"

"He has left Enriquez. Defected, he say to tell you. He will take you to the hideout and you can kill Enriquez."

"Where is Santos now?"

"I will take you to him. He is not far away."

Gunn considered it. He could be walking into a trap. An ambush. There was no way of telling. He believed the man in front of him, but he could have been duped by Santos. Still, he had no leads, no clear trail to Enriquez.

"Did Santos mention a man name of Morgan! Ethan Morgan?"

Pepe's head bobbed animatedly.

"Si. He knows where he is. He will take you to him."

"Let me get my boots on. You have a name?"

Pepe told him.

"You come with me, Pepe. And if you even look cross-eyed, I'll blow your bellybutton out your asshole."

I am very harmless, *Señor* Gunn. You will not have to shoot me. And Santos he is your friend."

"Yeah, I'll bet he is."

Gunn waved Pepe ahead of him toward the room. They had no sooner reached the door when Gunn heard a commotion on the stairs. He shoved Pepe inside and went into a crouch.

Two girls raced toward him.

"Gunn! Are you Gunn?"

"I am," he said. "You're waking up the whole hotel."

"Help us, quick! Someone is after us!"

Elena Sutter ran up to Gunn, her eyes wide with fright. Behind her, Junia Diaz panted, her hair askew, her eyes equally wide.

"Hold on now," Gunn said. "What's all this about? I don't know you, but you know me. How come?"

"There's no time! We were followed. Let us in your room!" Elena looked toward the stairs, then screamed.

"He's coming, Elena!" shrieked Junia.

And Gunn heard it too. Boots on the stairs. Two at a time. And the girls blocked his way. If there was going to be shooting, someone was going to be killed.

Before he could push the girls out of the way, Eva burst into the hall.

"Gunn! For God's sake, what's going on?"

Before he could answer, Paco Loran cleared the top of the stairs. He had a rifle in his hand. He aimed it at Gunn, towering above the three women.

"Don't move, *Señor* Gunn!" Paco yelled. "I have got you dead in my sights!"

118

ELEVEN

"Drop the pistol!"

Paco Loran moved a step forward, rifle to his shoulder. He shoved the barrel toward Gunn, threatening him with the gesture.

Gunn's mind raced to make an instant decision.

The Mexican didn't have a clear shot, he knew. It was still dark in the hall, although some light had begun to seep through the window at his back. He probably made a good enough target, even so. The girls had turned to face the man with the rifle and partially shielded him. Eva, too, was in the line of fire. To try for a shot would be to risk their lives needlessly. Yet to disarm himself would be sheer suicide. He would be at the intruder's mercy with no hope to get out alive.

The decision was a tough one.

Gunn made it and made it quick.

While the Mexican hesitated, Gunn ran to the wall, crouching and firing off-handed as he cleared the girls in front of him. The hall boomed with explosion. He saw flame and smoke belch from the rifle; heard the angry whine of the bullet as it seared the air.

The three women screamed in mortal terror.

White smoke filled the hallway.

Splinters of wood speared loose from the wall where the rifle's bullet plowed a six-inch furrow a foot from Gunn's head.

Paco Loran staggered.

Gunn's bullet reamed through the calf of the Mexican's leg. Paco levered the rifle and pain-crazed, fired again. Blindly.

Gunn hugged the wall, hammered back for a second shot at his attacker. Out of the corner of his eye, he saw Eva crumple, stumble. She screamed and the pain-filled cry bounced off the walls, ripped through the hall, agony in every shrill note.

Gunn fired again, squeezing the trigger with a hatred borne of vengeance and rage. He saw only smoke and flame, but he willed the bullet to strike home, to kill.

Eva fell to the floor and Gunn's anger boiled over in his brain. One of the girls, he couldn't see which, rushed to Eva's side. He saw her kneel down, the dusky-skinned one who had first approached him. He fought the impulse to rush over and comfort her. He turned his attention back to the man who had shot her, his gray eyes narrowed to malevolent slits.

The Mexican reeled backwards, vomiting blood. It spewed out of his open mouth in a crimson torrent, flecked with chunks of pink flesh. The rifle fell from his hands. He clutched his throat and Gunn saw the hole dead center in his chest, like a painted dot of red, growing larger as fresh blood gushed into it with every pump of his heart. The man fell to one knee, struggled to pull air into his shattered and collapsed lungs.

Blood continued to spew out of his mouth, pump from the hole in his chest.

Paco Loran fell over on his side, twitched. His mouth made horrible wheezing sounds. Bloody bubbles formed on his bluing lips.

The dying man stenched the air with a foul smell of gas and excrement as his sphincter muscle collapsed.

Gunn needed no further confirmation.

The man who had attacked him was dead. Or near it. He wouldn't get up again. He didn't know who the man was, but he had come to kill.

Eva groaned in pain.

Holstering his pistol, Gunn knelt down to see how badly she was hurt. Both girls, the strangers, were beside the wounded girl. Junia held one of Eva's hands. Elena pressed her thumb and forefinger, the half-circle of flesh between the two digits, down hard on a spot just above the wound.

Eva had a bloody groove in her thigh, just below the hip. A glance told Gunn that the wound was not serious, just painful. Her face was drawn, gray as the dawn light filtering through the hall of death. He saw that she had slipped into a dress but wore nothing underneath. He would never have sent the Mexican into the room if he'd known she was awake. The Mexican must have gone inside, surprised her. He might even have awakened her, yet he had heard no cry. At least she had managed to put something on before the shooting started.

The wound was fairly clean. Gunn looked carefully at the bloody furrow to see if pieces of cloth had clung to the flesh. There were none. The wound would have to be cleansed in case there were particles of lead or other matter that could cause an infection.

There was no sign of the Mexican, so he was probably still in the room.

"You did fine," Gunn told the girl who was putting pressure on Eva's thigh to staunch the bleeding. "Let's move her inside, get some alcohol, hot water, bandages, a salve. No telling who'll be coming up those stairs next."

So far, no one had come to investigate the gunfire. Gunn could only assume that people were either used to guns going off at all hours, or that they were just too damned scared to find out what all the ruckus was.

Gunn lifted Eva's shoulders. The two girls carried her by the legs. Eva was unconscious; a blessing, Gunn thought. She was light as a feather. They carried her inside the room, laid her on the bed.

"I'll get the medicine," said Junia.

"Thanks," said Gunn.

A head peeked up from behind the bed.

Pepe.

"Who's that?" asked Elena.

"He won't hurt you. Come on out," Gunn told the Mexican. "It's all over."

Pepe, wearing a sheepish look on his face, stood up. He looked at Eva, saw the bared leg, the wound. He crossed himself.

"I was very afraid," he said. "I heard the shooting."

"Just stay close. We'll go find Santos when we get this girl fixed up."

"Santos?" Elena spat. "What business do you have with that snake?"

Gunn pulled the shades, letting in the morning light.

"He's supposed to lead me to this girl's father. A man named Morgan."

Elena's eyes flashed fire. Gunn took a good look at her. She was sensual, fiery, earthy. Like a cat, he sensed that her claws were sharp. He liked her instantly.

"I am Elena Sutter," she said, 'and I have just come from the camp of Enriquez. He is holding Morgan a prisoner, making him work on the rifles, show his men how to work the new ones that were stolen from him. I was there when Santos came and told him about you. That is why my friend Junia Diaz and I ran away. To warn you, to ask you to help us. We have heard that you are very macho and that you have killed many men."

"I can't help you," he said. He pointed to Eva. "I have my hands full. And I want to free her father."

"But we can help you!" Elena pleaded. "We know everything about Enriquez. How many men, how many guns. We know where the camp is."

"There is a woman here who can care for your friend. Her name is Honora Bienvenidos. She knows much about healing. We will take her there and then you must take us to a safe place. When Jersey Slim finds out we are gone. . . ."

"Who's Jersey Slim?"

As Pepe listened intently, Elena told of her capture, her subjugation to Slim. She told Gunn of Enriquez's fear of the soldiers on his trail and how dangerous he was. As he listened, he knew that Elena was afraid of both Slim and Enriquez. She told him that the Mexican bandit leader was a man of no mercy. He believed her.

"Tell me about Pedro Santos," Gunn said.

"He is a snake."

"You said that. Is he leading me into a trap?"

"Yes. I'm sure of that. He works for Enriquez. But he is, underneath, a coward. He will be much afraid of you."

Gunn made up his mind as Elena poured water from the pitcher into a bowl and dabbed Eva's feverish face with a damp cloth. For Eva's sake, he had to try and free her father. He'd need to trust Santos to a certain extent, but he vowed to keep a sharp eye on him every step of the way.

Eva groaned when Elena started to dab at the fresh blood in the wound. Most of the heavy bleeding had stopped, thanks to the pressure applied by Elena. If properly treated, the blood would coagulate, seal off the small vessels and capillaries.

Junia Diaz arrived with Honora Bienvenidos, a bulky, wide-hipped woman in a flowered dress that covered her ankles. Her thick black hair was piled behind her head in massive coils held together by a large tortoise-shell comb. She carried a canvas satchel with her and began to attend to Eva instantly after shoving Gunn aside.

"My sons will be here soon," she said, "to carry this poor girl to my house. Someone is coming to clean up that mess in the hall. He was the man who shot this girl. And you shot him. Good! *Basura*. Trash. This town is full of trash."

The woman talked rapidly, but her conversation did not interfere with her work. Gunn saw that Eva was in good hands.

"Do you need me?" he asked. "Will she be all right?"

"She is in shock. She will be fine." The woman put two pillows under Eva's feet. She began to dress the wound expertly. "You are not needed. I am sure you do much better with the gun than with the bandage."

Gunn shifted his weight, slightly uncomfortable. He began looking around the room for his hat. He looked at Elena and Junia.

The eyes pleaded with him. He could not avoid them any longer.

"What about you two?" he asked.

Elena stepped up to him, looked up at his face.

"Let us stay here," she said. "Until you return."

"Can I get inside Enriquez's camp in daylight?"

Both girls shook their heads.

"Then I'll be back here right soon. You can stay here until then. I want to see this Pedro Santos first."

"He still works for Enriquez," Elena reminded him.

"Do not trust Santos," said Junia. "He will shoot you in the back."

Gunn cracked a wry grin.

"I have an idea," he said. "If it works, I can get Morgan out tonight."

"It will be very dangerous," said Elena. "Would you wear this for luck?" She reached up and pulled a thonged pendant from her neck. She put it around Gunn's neck. The pendant was a turquoise and silver thunderbird.

"I might not come back," Gunn said.

"You will. Watch out for Jersey Slim. He is a killer. He is much more dangerous than Enriquez."

"Thanks. I'll see you both before I go."

Impulsively, Elena stood on tiptoes and kissed Gunn on the cheek. He flushed with embarrassment. He backed away, looked over at Eva. She was still unconscious.

Junia came up, kissed him, too.

"How will you make Santos do what you want?" she asked.

"I'm going to make him trust me." Gunn said. "With his life."

The *jacal* was fenced, ringed with brush and cactus. It was almost invisible until Gunn rode up on it, following Pepe. The *jacal* was on the edge of town, set against a hillside, abandoned by some unknown Indian who had patiently thatched the roof, the walls. Gunn rode the claybank, Pepe sat atop the horse Gunn had bought for Eva. She wouldn't need it for a while. Pepe was nervous, jittery. Gunn made him dismount some distance from the *jacal* and approach it on foot. The hut appeared deserted, but there was a horse ground-tied out back.

Gunn dismounted, held the sorrel gelding so that he could use the animal for cover. The claybank mare covered his left flank, stood hip-shot. He watched Pepe walk unsteadily toward the fence that surrounded the hovel. If he followed the instructions Gunn had given him, he'd be all right. He wasn't to enter the enclosure of the *jacal,* but call Santos out. Then, he was supposed to tell Santos about the man Gunn now knew to be Paco Loren, one of those who had been on the raid with Lopez when the wagons had been stolen. If Santos was smart, he'd know that it would be best to cooperate, play it straight. Pepe was to tell Santos about the girls' escaping and one other thing: come out and talk, unarmed. If Santos did not drop his gunbelt at that moment, Gunn was going to kill him. He no longer had the patience to play games.

The shootings in town had made Gunn edgy. He didn't know who the enemy was, so every man he saw was the enemy. Enriquez had to have sympathizers in the town. He might be an outlaw, but the poor people had little use for the law, especially soldier law. Often it was they who hid the owlhoots out, fed them, provided them with horses and ammunition. They did this partially out of fear, partially out of contempt for the rich from whom the bandits often stole. A man was wise to watch his back in towns that sympathized with outlaws. In his case, everyone knew by now that he was after Enriquez. He had killed at least two of his men and another who was one of the townspeople. He could expect no help in Tres Piedras. On the contrary, he could expect another Cornejo at any time. There were those, too, who might turn outlaw, who would want to join up with a man like Enriquez and would not hesitate to shoot him dead if that would put them in good with the bandit leader. It was not a good situation, but he had to make the best of it.

Right now, Santos was the unknown factor. He was a lure, hired by Enriquez to draw him into the camp so he could be killed. What he had to do was turn the tables. Make Santos fear for his life so much that he wouldn't dare doublecross Gunn. Enriquez might have the numbers, but Gunn had the element of surprise in his favor. If he could penetrate the camp after nightfall, he stood a better chance than those inside the camp. They would be shooting at shadows. He would know that everyone there was a potential target. Everyone except Ethan Morgan. Before he went in, though, he would know every inch of the encampment. He would know who was where, what arms they had, something of their personalities. He would get this information from Santos, if he cooperated, and doublecheck that information with the two girls now in his hotel room.

Pepe called out to Santos in Spanish.

Silence.

Gunn bristled with wariness.

Pepe called again.

"I have brought Gunn here. He is here!"

From the *jacal*, an answer.

"Bring him inside!"

"No, you come out, Santos. I will talk with you."

Gunn could hear them clearly. He recognized the voice of the man he'd seen in the saloon when Lopez had made his play.

A long silence followed Pepe's querulous command.

Gunn stayed out of it. Let Pepe handle it. If Santos showed, and listened, fine. If he didn't, Gunn would ride out and let the man sweat. He wanted Pepe to tell Santos about Paco Loran, but Santos would find out anyway, if he lived that long. Patience was a thin thread at best. It could snap at any time. Gunn had had his fill of gunnies after his hide. Until he knew different, Santos was the enemy, just as everyone else he met from that point on was the enemy. It was a matter of survival. Simply that, and no more.

Santos appeared, suddenly, at the gate to the crude fence. He looped up the slope, saw Gunn standing behind the horses. It seemed to Gunn that he nodded.

There were no weapons in his hand.

"That is Gunn up there?" asked Santos loudly.

"Yes. He wants you to know that he just killed Paco Loran. Paco shot first."

"Paco dead?"

Pepe nodded.

"The fool!"

"Gunn says he will kill you too if you do not do what he says." Pepe didn't sound very convincing, Gunn thought. He was scared half out of his wits. But at least he got the point across.

"What does he want me to do?"

"He will tell you. Drop your gunbelt, now, Pedro, or he will shoot you."

"Now?"

"Real quick. He will kill you if he does not see the belt fall to the ground."

Gun saw Santos hesitate. He moved his own hand closer to his pistol. The morning sun was behind his back. Santos would be at a disadvantage.

Pepe started to shake.

"Hurry, Santos, the man is not joking."

"Is he going to shoot me after I drop my gun?" Santos asked, his voice even louder than before.

Gunn shook his head.

Pepe grinned with relief.

Santos moved his hands very slowly. He touched his belt buckle, the leather. A second later, the gunbelt slid to the ground.

"He did it, Gunn!" shouted Pepe. "You can come down now and talk to Santos."

"Step aside, Pepe!" Gunn said. He ground-tied the two horses, his eyes never leaving Santos. Something was wrong. He just couldn't put his finger on it. It was too easy.

Too damned easy.

"You alone, Santos?" Gunn called down to the man after the horses were tied. He looked down the slope, saw that the earth swelled into a small gully he couldn't see, then swelled again, making two small humps. All he had to do was walk down there and talk to Santos. Santos nodded.

Again, too easy.

Yet, Santos did not appear nervous. It was almost as if he had expected Gunn to disarm him. Maybe he had.

"I'm coming down," Gunn said. "Like Pepe said. To talk. I'm not going to shoot you."

Unless you do something funny, Gunn said to himself.

Gunn stepped away from the horses and started down the slope.

Santos did not move. Pepe watched him curiously.

Gunn couldn't shake off the feeling that something was wrong. His instincts for danger seemed especially keen as he stepped around a *nopal,* avoiding its spines. The hairs on the back of his neck prickled.

Clumps of cactus clung to the hillside. The Mexican women burned the spines off the *nopal,* sliced them into chunks which they put in their *chili con carne.* They were succulent, tasty, especially the young *nopales.* Gunn wasn't thinking of them that way, but as cover for someone who didn't want to be seen. His eyes scanned those nearby, but he could detect nothing out of place. Still, the feeling persisted that all was not right.

The gully was no more than a game trail cutting

between the two humps of earth.

He started to step across it when a man rose up from behind a cactus.

The man was the ugliest Gunn had ever seen.

He was dressed like an Apache; naked, except for a loincloth, soft deerskin boots that were wrapped with leather thongs, a knife and a .44. His body was covered with the red dust of the earth so that he had been invisible lying behind the clump of *nopal*. His face was twisted under his cheekbone. His eye on that side was off-center, malevolent. His other eye was steady, glinting.

Even as Gunn went into a crouch, he knew it was too late.

He heard the man's hammer cock. The *click* filled the silence as the sear slid into place.

"I wouldn't try it if I was you," said the man.

Gunn froze.

He knew that Santos and Pepe couldn't see either of them. But they could hear.

"Who in hell are you?" asked Gunn.

"They call me Jersey Slim. I been waitin' fer you, Gunn. Didn't trust that Santos none and I see I was right. You got him buffaloed, but your string just run out."

Slim strode toward him and was on Gunn before he knew the man's intentions.

A hand shot out, jerked the thunderbird off his neck with a yank. The leather broke, but Gunn pitched forward. He heard a crack and everything went dark.

TWELVE

As Gunn fell toward him, Jersey Slim slammed the butt of his pistol down. The butt smashed into the back of Gunn's head. He went down like a sack of meal.

Slim laughed.

"Santos, get your ass down here!" he shouted.

He looked down at the thunderbird in his hand, cursed softly.

Santos and Pepe came running over the top of the rise. Santos was struggling into his gunbelt. Pepe was wide-eyed, confused.

Norris looked up at the two men.

"Jersey Slim, you are here! Did you kill the *gringo?*"

"Naw, killin's too good for this bastard. He got my gal and he'll pay. . . ."

Slim stopped, looked at Pepe.

"Who's this jasper, Santos?"

"He is just a friend who was helping me."

"Likely Gunn's friend, you mean." Norris raised his pistol, aimed it at Pepe.

"No, don't shoot me!" screamed Pepe. "I have done nothing!"

Santos turned pale.

Slim pulled the trigger. Pepe's face disappeared in a cloud of blood. He didn't even scream as his body flopped into a cluster of cactus. His body thrashed for a few seconds then was still.

Smoke curled up lazily from the barrel of Slim's pistol.

"Why did you shoot him? He was not dangerous."

Slim fixed his bad eye on Santos. Santos cringed. He shrank away from the look of the "evil eye."

"Good thing I come checkin' on you, Santos. You was about to make a bad mistake. I heard purt near everything, tried to make some sense on it."

"Slim, I was doing just what Enriquez told me to do. He wanted me to make friends with this Gunn, get him out to the canyon hideout so he could kill him. You did not have to check on me."

"Droppin' your gunbelt wasn't part of the deal! Why, it's a good thing I put his lamp out. He was probably gonna dust you off permanent."

Santos shrugged.

"Now, looky here," said Slim, holding up the thunderbird amulet. "How you figger this jasper got him a pretty I give to Elena?"

"I do not know."

"Onliest way is if she give it to him. She's gone and Paco's gone. So is Junia Diaz. Looks to me like Enriquez got troubles we don't even know about. You too, if you get my meanin'."

"I have done nothing wrong!" Santos insisted.

Slim fixed him with a hard glare.

"You think on it, Santos," Slim drawled. "Was I you I wouldn't go back out to the hideout. I got to give

Enriquez a report and he ain't gonna like you droppin' your gunbelt none. And takin' up with this Mexican weasel." Slim pointed the thunderbird at Pepe's body sprawled in the cactus. Blood oozed from a dozen spots where cactus spines had penetrated the skin.

"Where will I go? What will I do?"

"That's up to you, Santos. I aim to work this old boy over and feed him to the buzzards. If I see you again, I'm likely to fly off the handle. You like to see if you can beat me?"

Santos did not. He began edging away from Jersey Slim. He backed up the slope, watching as Slim bent down and crossed Gunn's hands behind his back. He knew what he was going to do. It was a favorite sport of Slim's. He was going to drag Gunn behind his horse. Through the cactus, over the rocks. There wouldn't be much left of Gunn when Slim got through with him. Santos shuddered, cleared the rise and began to run toward his horse in back of the *jacal*.

Slim was *loco*. He was a crazy killer. No one was safe around him. There had been no reason to shoot Pepe. But Slim was in a killing mood. Santos shivered to think what Slim would do to Gunn over that girl, Elena. Enriquez would not object. As long as Gunn was dead. But Slim had forgotten one thing. The girl, Morgan's daughter. Enriquez wanted her. And she had not come out with Gunn. That meant she was still in town. If he could find her, bring her back. . . .

Gunn woke up.

Someone was slapping his face. Hard. He opened

134

his eyes.

The hideous face leered at him. Jersey Slim. Enriquez's *segundo*.

Gunn felt the thongs around his wrists. They were wet, pulling up taut in the heat of the sun as they dried. He looked up, saw that he had been out for about fifteen minutes. His feet were not tied. Only his hands, behind his back. He moved his fingers. The leather was strong.

"Get the idea, pilgrim?" Slim leered. "We're gonna have us a drag party. I didn't want you to miss out, so I slapped you awake. You savvy?"

Gunn said nothing. He stared at Slim with steely blue-gray eyes.

"Give you a chance't, first though. I asked you once, about my woman, Elena. Where you got her?"

Gunn took the slap, let his head roll with it so that the impact wasn't so great. Slim's hand stung though. He felt nausea building up in his stomach. He saw, as his head twisted, the sprawled hulk of Pepe in the cactus clump. There was a hole where his nose met his forehead. The hole swarmed with the shiny green and blue bodies of flies.

"She come to you, didn't she?" There was saliva bubbling at the corners of Slim's mouth. His good eye glittered like an agate. His bad eye was wide, bloodshot. "You put the boots to her?"

Gunn braced himself for the next blow.

But none came.

Instead, Slim stood up, whistled. A horse came running up over the rise, trailing its reins. It stopped a few feet away. Slim untied the thongs around a bundle back of the cantle. His clothes. He put them on, taking his time as Gunn assessed the situation.

Jersey Slim was a madman. Further, he thought that Gunn had taken his girl. It would do no good to reveal to him where she was. Slim would likely kill once he got the information he sought. The only chance he had was to hang on, keep his mouth shut and try to catch Slim off-guard. If he survived the dragging, he had a chance. Not much of one, but a chance. Slim would show no mercy. Gunn saw that in the man's torn face, the cock-eye. He wondered now how he would have fared if Elena hadn't given him the amulet. He might have been shot down on the spot. And where was Santos? Pepe was dead. Why, Gunn didn't know. He had been harmless. Slim probably had blamed him for bringing Gunn out there. It was a puzzle. Maybe Santos had lit a shuck when he heard Slim's voice. Smart man. If so, then Santos might find Eva, and the other two girls in his room. Somehow, he had to get free, go back to town and hide the girls out. Guard Eva. He shuddered to think of how she might fare in the hands of a man like Jersey Slim.

The lanky man finished dressing, hung on his gun belt and knife and tied one end of the lariat around the saddle horn. He tied the other end to the front of Gunn's belt, on the buckle.

"One last chance't, pilgrim. You gonna tell me where my gal is?"

Gunn glared at Slim. He neither shook his head nor replied.

Slim's bad eye flared with anger. He swung up into the saddle, put the spurs to his horse's flanks. He horse was a big-boned Morgan mixed with Arabian. He looked as if he could get right down to it. Gunn braced himself. His only chance would be to keep his head up and ride his backside. The rope wasn't new, which was a factor in his favor. There was always the chance it might fray or get cut on a sharp stone.

Slim had taken his pistol so he was unarmed.

The buckskins would help some.

The horse took up the slack, kept going.

Gunn was jerked down, rolled so that he rode on his back. He bent his neck as far as he could. The horse picked up speed. He heard Slim yelling at it, snatches of words floating back to him. The brush and cactus went by at blurring speed. His hat protected his head from raking mesquite. His hands banged against small pebbles, but he managed to hold them next to his side, although the pain in his arm and shoulder was intense from the strain.

Slim looked back a time or two, then spurred his horse to a faster pace.

Gunn held his hands so that the thongs took most of the punishment. He felt his bonds loosen and began wriggling his wrists, trying to get them free of the thongs. He smelled something burning and knew that the fibers were heating up from the friction.

Slim reined his horse into a zig-zag pattern, trying for rougher terrain. Gunn winced as he tore through a *nopal.* Spines stabbed into his rump and legs. The cactus shattered into pulp and Gunn dug in his boot heels to slow himself down. The horse would have to work harder now and Gunn's rump was slightly elevated.

On an open stretch, Gunn bore down on the thongs around his wrists, felt them give. The smell of blood was raw in his nostrils. One hand came free and he twisted awkwardly as his arm flopped loose. With a wrench, he jerked the other hand free and brought his arms up, trying to grasp the rope tied to Slim's saddle horn.

Slim began to slap his horse, urging it to gain more speed. Gunn managed to grasp the rope. He pulled himself over so that he was sledding on one leg. Chunks of stone, splinters of brush scraped his flesh under the buckskin legging. He twisted again, sacrificing the other leg to the brutal pounding. Gunn drew up his leg and offered less skin to the drag. His arms and wrists ached from holding on to the tow rope. He held his head up, ducked when he saw brush in his way. He narrowly missed a large rock, twisting desperately at the last moment to avoid having his head crushed like an eggshell.

The horse began to tire. Running uphill, the animal stumbled, slowed. Despite Slim's vicious gouging with spurs, the horse couldn't regain its former speed. Gunn saw a chance to get free and take Slim down a notch or two. If he could swing wide, work the rope, he might be able to unseat Slim from the saddle.

There was another possibility, too. If Gunn could somehow manage to unbuckle his belt, he could be free of the rope. It was pure hell to concentrate, and he'd have to let go of the rope, work with both hands while crashing around through the brush. It would be a miracle if he could do it. But Slim was going to tire of his game soon and then he might start shooting.

Gunn saw still another opportunity a few seconds later. Slim was dragging him toward a small clump of rocks. If Gunn could get the rope through two of them, he might stop the horse. That would give him a few seconds to get his belt off and free of the drag rope.

He pulled up hard on the rope, drew himself to a sitting position. Spreading his legs wide, he dug in his boot heels. There was enough slack in the rope so that he could whip it up and over the rocks. His hands were raw and bleeding, but the rope sailed up and between the crevice of two rocks. The rocks came up fast and Gunn summoned up his last ounce of effort to dig in before the impact. At the last moment, he loosened his grip on the rope and threw himself backwards, his heels furrowing through the earth. His feet took the impact which wasn't as bad as he had expected.

Then he saw why.

The rope, going through the crevice, had weakened. When the horse took up the slack, the rope broke. Gunn hit the rocks with a *whump!* The air in his lungs was forced out by the rock hitting his stomach. Bile rose up in this throat. With raw fingers he forced his buckle open. His belt came free and he felt sick all over, as if he'd been stung by bees and run over by a wagon. His pain was split up, throbbed in every part of his body. He fought off the nausea; swallowed the bile, gritted his teeth.

He heard Slim yell, knew he would be back to check on him in a few seconds.

Hurling the belt and rope down, Gunn fell on his face, played dead.

He closed his eyes. And waited.

Slim approached him warily, still on horseback. Gunn heard the sounds of the horse's hooves, the wheeze of its lungs. The horse snorted. Gunn held fast, unmoving. He held his breath, hoping the Slim would think he was dead.

"Gunn? You hear me?"

Gunn's lungs ached, but he continued to hold his breath. Fire burned in the sacs, suffocating him. He felt as if he was going to burst if he didn't let the air out quick.

Leather creaked as Slim swung out of the saddle.

His boots clattered on the stones. Gunn heard the whisper soft sound of a pistol slipping out of its leather holster. He waited for the ominous click of the hammer thumbing back.

The boots stopped, inches from Gunn's head.

One of them prodded Gunn's ribs.

"I'll be a sum'bitch," muttered Slim. "Bastard's done gone and got kilt."

Gunn heard the thunk of the pistol slamming back into its holster.

He opened one eye to a slit. Saw Slim's boot six inches away. As it turned, he opened his eye wide, lashed out with his arm. He grabbed the boot, pushed, pulled. At the end of the pull, he twisted, wrenching Slim off balance.

With an oath, Slim clawed for his pistol.

Gunn scrambled to his feet, rushed Slim with the raging fury of a wild animal suddenly unloosed. He roared savagely, exulting in the fresh lungful of air, plowed into Slim's midsection, bowling him over. Slim's pistol hung half-way out of the holster. As he hit the ground, the pistol fell from his grasp. Gunn brought a knee up hard into Slim's groin.

Slim yelled in pain.

Gunn felt a fist slam against his ear. A slender arm, strong as a whip, coiled around his neck.

The two men rolled, each seeking an advantage.

Gunn dug a thumb into Slim's good eye.

Slim screamed, jerked his head. Gunn lost his grip, felt his back smash into a large stone as Slim rolled on top of him. A hand grasped his neck, squeezed the windpipe.

Gunn looked up into the hideous twisted face of the lanky gunman.

His air shut off. He could make no sound. The pressure from Slim's hand increased and Gunn started to lose consciousness.

With the last ounce of strength, Gunn shot his arm upward, fist doubled. His fist cracked into the jutting point of Slim's chin, driving his head backward. His grip on Gunn's neck slacked enough so that Gunn could breathe. Without waiting for Slim to recover from the blow, Gunn raised his head, grabbed Slim's arm and sank his teeth into the wrist. He heard bones snap as Slim's scream threatened to rupture his eardrums.

Slim kicked out, hard.

His boot caught Gunn in the side. After the battering he'd taken on the rope, it scarcely hurt. Some wind was knocked out of his lungs, but he felt stronger than before. Slim got to his feet, wavered unsteadily. Gunn got up just as fast, squared off before his adversary. Slim's good eye leaked water over his cheek and his bad eye looked like the red eye of a demon as he glared at Gunn.

For long seconds the men stared at each other, panting for breath. Slim's glance wavered. Gunn followed it and saw the pistol, lying there in the dust. He lunged for it.

Too late he saw his mistake.

Slim didn't make a move for the pistol.

Instead, he drew his knife, a modified Bowie with a wicked blade.

Gunn saw the flash of the blade out of the corner of his eye. The sun glinted off the cold white steel as Slim raised it hip-high and jabbed at Gunn's side. Gunn felt the tip slide across skin, felt the rush of warm blood. He twisted away before the blade could sink in, fell flat on his face. His hand stretched inches from the barrel of Slim's pistol.

With a cry of triumph, Slim dove at Gunn, the knife raised high.

Gunn saw and heard him coming.

If he moved for the pistol, he'd have to eat about eight inches of steel. Rolling over fast, Gunn brought his legs up double. Slim's momentum carried him toward the spot where Gunn had been a split-second before. Too late, he tried to twist and bury the knife in Gunn's belly. Gunn kicked out hard with both feet. His boots caught Slim in the hip, knocked him sideways.

Slim jolted to the ground, slid a half a foot, an expression of surprise on his twisted face.

His left hand went behind him, closed around the butt of his pistol.

Gunn got to his feet, his fists doubled up.

Slim held him at bay with the knife while he brought the pistol around, cocked it.

"Looks like this is where you buy it, pilgrim," Slim said.

Sweat poured down Gunn's face. He stood there, legs apart, his fists clamped tight.

He looked into the black hole of the barrel.

A grin of satisfaction broke over Slim's face.

His finger tightened on the trigger.

THIRTEEN

Gunn sucked in a breath.

It would be over soon. For him, or for Slim. Maybe both of them.

Slim gloated as his finger tightened on the trigger.

Gunn smiled.

It wasn't over yet. Slim thought it was, but he was wrong. He had both hands full and both eyes open.

Gunn broke into a laugh.

"Damn you!" shrieked Slim, "what the hell you laughin' at?"

Gunn opened his fists, flung the dirt in them straight at Slim's face. At his eyes.

Then he dove for the ground.

The pistol went off with a roar. Smoke and flame spewed from the barrel. Gunn heard the slug whistle over his head. He got up in an instant, saw Slim helplessly rubbing his eyes with the backs of both hands. His hands held pistol and knife. The lid of the good eye was clamped shut. The bad eye was a twisted slit, running with fluid and red dirt.

"That's why I was laughing, you sonofabitch!" Gunn

said, kicking Slim hard in the side of the head. He reached down, snatched the pistol from Slim's hand, ground his boot heel into the other. The knife fell out of Slim's agonized grip. A bone snapped. It was the same wrist Gunn had bitten. It now dangled like a dead thing from the end of the killer's arm. Gunn kicked the knife away, out of reach.

Gunn hammered the pistol back, stepped back four paces.

He watched Slim grovel in pain, trying to claw the dirt out of his eyes.

There was time now to catch his breath. He picked up the blade, shoved it in his belt. He hurt all over, but he didn't mind the pain anymore. He had won. He had beaten Jersey Slim against all odds. It didn't often happen that way. He was lucky.

Slim half-sat, favoring his broken wrist. Tears streamed down his face. He looked even more hideous than before. Streaks of red dirt lines coursed down his cheeks. His flesh was purpled where Gunn's blows had scored.

Gunn's instincts told him he had a worse problem now.

What do you do with a captured rattlesnake?

Jersey Slim would have shown him no mercy, had the tables been turned. Yet Gunn could not kill a man in cold blood. Slim had lost and he was still alive. He was now disarmed and had a broken wrist to boot. To shoot a man in such a situation would be no less than cowardly.

But something had to be done with Slim. He was still a dangerous man. A killer. Some of the starch had been taken out of him, but he'd recover.

Gunn needed to keep him out of action for a while without killing him.

The idea came to him as he rubbed his wrists. The rope had left deep raw welts where it had cut into the skin.

An eye for an eye. A tooth for a tooth.

As for himself, Gunn needed rest, a bath, fresh clothes.

"Take off your boots, Norris," Gunn said quietly.

"Huh?"

"You heard me. Shuck off those boots if you want to keep what's left of your hide."

Slim looked at the barrel of his own pistol. Gunn's hand was steady. The aim dead on his good eyebrow. He apparently decided that Gunn wasn't bluffing. He struggled with one boot, unlacing the thongs, working it off his foot with his good hand.

"Now the other one," Gunn said.

"What do you aim to do, pilgrim?"

"Slow you down some."

"You gonna shoot me?"

"I might. You could use some extra weight."

Slim's face paled, but he showed no sign of begging for his life. His socks were dirty.

"Toss me the boots," Gunn told him.

Slim picked up a boot, tossed it. Then the other.

"Good boots. Apache?"

"I took 'em off'n an Apache," Slim grinned.

Gunn bent down, tied the thongs together, slung the boots over his shoulder.

"Get up," he said.

Slim struggled to his feet. His broken wrist dangled at his side. He winced with the sudden pain as the blood rushed to the extremity of the broken bones.

"Now whistle that horse of yours in," Gunn said.

"You ain't gonna take my horse."

"Like hell I'm not. You're going to walk back. Carrying a load."

When Slim hesitated, Gunn fired a round at his feet. The bullet kicked up dirt and rocks, sprayed Slim's feet and legs.

He whistled for his horse.

The big Arabian/Morgan trotted up close. Gunn grabbed the reins.

"Slip off your gunbelt."

Slim dropped his gunbelt. Gunn gestured and he kicked it over to Gunn. Gunn threw it across the saddle.

"Now walk back to that cactus where Pepe is." As Slim started limping off, Gunn followed, leading the horse. The rope attached to the saddle horn dragged behind the horse.

"Lie on your belly," Gunn commanded as they halted next to the cactus where Pepe's body was sprawled, ripening in the sun.

"What for?"

"Move it, Slim, or join the cactus flower there."

Slim lay face down on the earth. Gunn grabbed his good wrist and twisted it behind his back.

"Put your other hand back there," said Gunn. "Cross 'em over real nice."

Slim did as he was told. Gunn strapped on Slim's gunbelt, holstered his pistol. Then he cut a short length of line from the drag rope with Slim's knife. He put his boot in the small of Slim's back.

"Move, and you're dead, Norris."

Gunn dropped his knee to Slim's back, pinning him

down at the same spot where his boot had been. He began tying the man's wrists together, leaving plenty of rope left over to truss his arms. He tied the knots so that the more Slim struggled, the tighter they would draw. When he was satisfied, Gunn stood up. He wasn't finished yet.

He cut a longer length of rope from the lariat, laid it alongside the bound man. Then Gunn went to the cactus and lifted the dead body of Pepe out of the *nopal.* The blood had dried and the body was stiff.

"Get to your knees," Gunn told Slim.

"You ain't gonna. . . ."

"Get to your knees!"

Gunn tied the dead body to Slim's back. Slim boiled with anger. The stench of death gagged him. He vomited twice and it was all Gunn could do to avoid spilling his own guts. He finished the knots, checked them, and stepped away.

"Stand up," he ordered. Slim struggled to his feet. Pepe's body draped over his shoulders.

"You fuckin' bastard!" Slim muttered.

"Listen, Slim, you got three choices as I see it. You can stay here and struggle with that dead body and die of thirst. It's going to be blazing hot all day long. You can go back to your hideout and answer a whole hell of a lot of embarrassing questions. Or, you can go into Tres Piedras and get somebody to cut Pepe off your back. Anyway you do, you walk, carrying him with you."

"I'll get you for this, Gunn."

Gunn laughed and grabbed up Slim's horse. He climbed into the saddle, hauled up the canteen. As Slim watched, he worked the cork loose and drank deeply. Slim cursed silently, glaring at Gunn like a man crucified.

"Oh, one other thing," Gunn said before he rode away to gather up the other two horses, "if you go into town, I'll put you in the same grave with Pepe there."

Gunn rode away slowly, never looking back.

★ ★ ★

Santos drew deep on the marijuana cigarette.

It was the first he'd had in a long time. Brought up from the mountain fields of Guerrero. The smoke relaxed him, dulled his brain.

Still, he managed to smile when he saw Gunn ride into town leading two horses.

One of them he recognized as Jersey Slim's.

He was not very surprised to see Gunn alive.

The man was not human. That is, he was human, but he had the shadow following him. There were such men he knew. *Hombres de sombra.* These were the ones who always seemed to have the good luck. They escaped death seemingly without effort because they were protected by the shadow. He had heard of such men but had never seen one until now. It was truly an awesome thing.

The last he'd seen of Gunn, Slim had been in command. Anyone else would be dead by now. He knew Slim. Knew of his meanness, his burning anger at the world. Sim thought no more of killing a man that he did of swatting a fly or crushing a toad underfoot. He was a man without shame or conscience.

Yet there was no sign of Slim.

Only his horse.

Santos felt his stomach fall open, like a bottomless pit.

Gunn was back, wearing Slim's gunbelt, leading the Arabian/Morgan. Slim would never willingly part with such a horse. Nor would any man give up his personal weapons without a fight.

Gunn had been in a fight. He looked bad. His face wore a scowl, and was comparatively unmarked. But his buckskins were in tatters. Blood smeared on the sleeves, the trousers worn through. Santos saw bloody patches of leg.

Gunn had not noticed him and Santos didn't want to be seen by him. Not yet. He drew into the shadows between two buildings and watched as Gunn rode up to the livery stable He was not surprised to see him emerge a few minutes later and head for the hotel.

Santos followed at a safe distance.

Somehow, he knew, Gunn was the answer to his own fate.

Only he knew where Morgan's daughter was.

And Enriquez wanted the girl, along with Gunn.

★ ★ ★

Gunn ordered a bath drawn for him when he got back to the hotel.

Then he went straight for his room.

"You look like forty mile of bad road," exclaimed Elena when she let him inside.

"What happened?" asked Junia.

"Jersey Slim Norris."

Elena paled. Her eyes flew to his neck, saw that the thunderbird was gone.

"Did he. . . .did you. . . .?"

149

"Not now," he said. "I'm just one big sore spot and they're drawing me a bath downstairs. You gals don't have much to worry about for a while though. Far as I know, Slim didn't even know you were gone until he spotted that silver trinket you gave me."

Elena turned away from him, embarrassed.

Gunn began to peel out of his shirt. What was left of it. His muscles were tender, bruised. There were deep raw scratches in his flesh where the rocks and plants had plowed over him.

Nothing broken.

There were a lot of questions Gunn had for the girls, but those could wait, too. He wanted to know if anyone had come around asking about Paco Loran and who had killed him. He wondered if Elena had set him up. She hadn't mentioned being Slim's girl. That had almost gotten him killed. She seemed genuinely upset, but he didn't know if that was becasue he had showed up instead of Slim or because he looked so damned bad. Both girls oohed and aahed when they saw him naked. Neither seemed disturbed that he had stripped down in front of them. Being from a bandit's band, they had seen worse, he figured.

The bath was a luxury. He soaked the ache out of his muscles, let the warm water restore his spirits if not his flesh. There wasn't anything wrong with him that wouldn't heal in time. He still wanted to break into Enriquez's camp and get Ethan Morgan free. His plans would have to be altered however. He didn't know where in hell Santos was, but he sure as hell needed him now. Since he didn't know Slim was walking a dead man back to Enriquez's, he had probably lit a shuck. Or, he might still be around.

150

Back in the room, he found one of his answers.

He was here," said Junia, excited. "We talked to him."

"Who?" asked Gunn.

"Santos!" both girls said in unison.

"He wants to see you. He says he will still take you to the camp. He has quit Enriquez." Elena seemed genuinely pleased. Both girls had taken time to put on rouge, comb their hair, pretty up. He stood there, a huge towel wrapped around his muscular frame, towering above them. His hair was slick wet, clung to his skull.

"Where? When?"

"Later on, in the plaza. He wants no trouble." Elena seemed certain.

"One of you girls want to take those old buckskins down to the dry goods and get me some duds that are about the same size. Anything cool and wearable. I got some riding to do."

Gunn fished out some bills from his possibles bag. Junia stuck out her hand.

"I will do it," she said. "I have felt like a bird in a cage all day.

"Pants, shirt, some socks."

"How about some underwear?" asked Junia.

"Seldom bother with it. One more thing to wash." He grinned as Junia's face flushed with embarrassment. That surprised him a little. She might have been a rough girl, but she was still a woman clean through. He liked her. He like both of them, but Junia was not as complex as Elena. She had the look of a hawk about her, the proud mien of a gypsy. He could see why Slim had been attracted to her. She was half-wild, still, and he must have had a thought or two about her loyalty. He was sure she had a story or two to tell.

"I'll be back soon," said Junia.

"Take your time," said Elena, pointedly.

Junia nodded as if she understood.

Gunn didn't.

"Be careful," he told her. "I still don't trust Santos."

"Oh, he's not lying. He is a snake and I could tell if he was lying. He said you probably killed Jersey Slim."

"Did you?" asked Elena.

"No, but he's probably wishing I did," said Gunn.

After Junia left, Gunn lay on the bed, the towel still wrapped around his mid-section.

Across the room, Elena watched him with those hawk eyes of hers. Gunn closed his eyes, weary.

"She won't be back for a while, you know." Elena spoke after several long seconds of silence.

"Huh?"

"Junia. She knows I wanted to be alone with you for a while. I locked the door."

Gunn opened his eyes, groaned.

"Elena, I'm not a whole man. I hurt something fierce."

"I can make the pain go away."

She glided across the room toward him, unbuttoning her blouse. Gunn looked at her through half-lidded eyes.

"Some other time," he said. "The spirit is willing, but the flesh is mighty weak."

Elena bared her breasts.

Gunn stared at them.

Beauties. Pert saucy nipples jutting out of dark

aureoles. Firmly uptilted. Beckoning. He felt a stir at his loins.

Elena stood there, unhooked her skirt. Let it fall to the floor with a whisper of cloth.

"Do you like me?" she asked, her voice husky with desire.

Gunn swallowed.

Her body was flawless. The dusky olive skin was smooth as velvet. The thatch between her legs a beckoning mystery. Her long hair flowed over soft shoulders.

"I reckon. Some."

Elena reached down, snatched away the towel. Gunn winced as cloth rubbed across painful scratches.

"You do like me," she squealed. "Just look at you! *Hombre. Hombron!*"

Gunn looked down at himself.

Elena was right.

His liking for her showed.

FOURTEEN

Elena surprised him again.

With her boldness.

She hopped into bed, curled up at his feet and bent over, taking his half-hard bone in her hands. She began kissing the crown, licking the tender flesh with her flicking tongue. He felt a searing stab of desire as her tongue lingered over the tiny mouthlike slit.

His manhood grew rapidly.

Her fingers caressed the swelling stalk as her mouth opened wider. She placed her lips gently around the flaring mushroomed head, pulled it into the steaming moistness of her mouth. Gunn's spine jangled with ten thousand volts of electricity. As if lightning had struck him.

His loins flooded with warmth.

He reached out for her, touched fingers to her cheek.

"Umm," she moaned. "Sweet. *Muy dulce.*"

Gunn forgot about his bruises, the angry welts, the weariness. His body surged with strength.

Elena's cheeks collapsed as she suckled him, drawing

his organ deep into her mouth, soaking it with warm saliva. She was expert in her oral manipulations. Gunn slid fingers through her hair, massaged her scalp. She drew him deeper, into her throat. He felt as if he would explode at that moment. Her lips pressed right around the swollen member, tightened down on the engorged veins. The pressure built up like steam in an engine boiler. Her breasts hung down from her chest, the nipples thrust out hard. Hung there appealingly until he wanted to draw her body up to his and crush her against him.

But the pleasure was too intense.

"It's good, Elena," he said. "Damned good."

"Mmmmmmf," she replied.

Gunn suppressed a laugh as she slid his cock in and out of her, bobbing up and down on it like some devouring creature. Whoever had taught her, had taught her well.

Faster and faster she bobbed, ramming him deep down her throat, her lips drawn tight around his manhood.

Gunn understood.

She wanted him to come. In her mouth.

It was a rare pleasure.

Most women stopped short of that. For some reason. But Elena wanted his seed. Wanted it all. She told him that with the energy of her exertions. Her breasts rose up and down, the nipples touching his leg, brushing against the fine hairs. He felt his seed boil, threaten to explode. He put his hands on her head, held her in a caress as his excitement raced through flesh and bone.

"Now!" he said, gripping her head tightly.

Elena stopped, created powerful suction with her mouth.

Gunn exploded.

He felt his seed rush up his stalk in unrestrained release.

It was a moment of incredible joy and power. Of exquisite beauty. Elena looked up at him with smoky eyes. Glistening eyes bright as a ferret's at the kill. The floodtide of pleasure engulfed him, swept him up to dizzy heights, took his breath away in a whirlwind of raw, strong feeling.

The hurt came when she spewed him out of her mouth.

The brush of her lips across the tender crown of his manhood was exquisitely painful. He winced and reached for her. She flowed into his arms. Their lips met and his hungry tongue explored her mouth. He tasted himself and her and the twinges in his loins kept coming even as his power waned, as his stiffness subsided.

"Ah," he breathed, and crushed her close to him. Crushed her breasts against his massive chest and breathed her scent. Breathed of her hair and her female scent, her womanly musk, the fresh clean breath from her loving mouth. It was a sweet moment and Gunn didn't want to lose it. He wondered, then, who she was and where she had come from and why. He roamed fingers over her smooth back and down the curve of her spine. Touched the gentle slopes of her buttocks and the contours of her sides. Felt her meld against him in a natural way, fitting into his concavity perfectly. "Ah," he said again and smothered her with another kiss, a deeper one that tasted of lemon and the sea.

She nestled in his arms, resting her head on his

broad chest. He put his arms around her naked back. She felt good there. Natural. Female as a purring kitten. The bruises and scrapes did not hurt now. He was aware of them, but he could almost feel his body healing. He was relaxed, at peace with himself and with the world.

"I want you inside me," she whispered. "As soon as you can."

"I can. Anytime."

She raised her head, looked into his pale gray-blue eyes. A look of surprise etched in her features.

"Really?"

"Feel for yourself."

She touched him. He was half-hard still.

"How do you do that?" Her voice was full of wonder.

"You do it," he said.

Elena laughed, squeezed his manhood. She ran her fingers up and down, over the distended blue veins, down to the scrotum. She hefted the sac, weighed it in her small hand. Her fingers traced a path around his groin, slid beneath him to caress his buttocks. He felt the touch, light as a feather, and the heat began to flood back into his loins. His spine started to tingle. There was something about the way she touched him that excited him, brought back memories. Memories of Laurie. His wife. Slain in the beauty of her youth. Slain senselessly. But he didn't think of her as being dead, but as being part of every woman he met. Part of Elena, even, although there were no superficial similarities. Just the way she touched him, explored his body with the tips of her fingers. Like Laurie.

Her hand slid down his brawny leg, rubbed the knee as if it was another sexual organ. Caressed the underside of it as if stroking his hard bare cock. Elena was good. She knew how to please a man. His organ rose with every new venture of her hand, her fingers. Hardened into horn.

Her finger made tiny whorls on the crown of his cock, each touch shooting electric charges through his flesh, into his veins. She stretched the loose folds of uncircumcised skin back, revealing the bullet-headed mass that she had so recently suckled to orgasm. Gunn felt a deep twinge as his cock began to throb with fresh blood.

"I like your body," she said, her voice like a child's, far away, dreamy. "All of it, not just this part." She touched one of his bruises. Touched it so gently he scarcely felt it. Soothing fingers roamed over the skinned parts of his legs and hips. She leaned over, kissed a welt on his side. The kiss a soft delicate thing like the faint brush of a spider web. Something inside him began to melt and flow and he remembered his youth and the pretty girls that caught his eye in the green Arkansas summers when the Osage flowed quiet in the Blue Hole and they swam naked and free, diving off the bluffs into the deep cool water.

As he lay there, her hands soothed over every inch of his body, played with the locks of his hair and tingled inside his ears. She spoke not at all, but seemed absorbed with his body as if she had never seen a naked man before. He lay there, pleased and excited, because she was doing it all on her own without any urging from him.

"I'm exploring you," she said finally. "I want to feel your weight on me. Just touching you makes me excited. Did any woman ever explore you like this before?"

"Not like this."

"But someone did." Was she pouting? He wasn't sure.

"My wife. Laurie."

"Ah, your wife."

"She's dead."

"Dead. How sad."

"Yes."

"But she explored you. Did you explore her like this?"

Gunn felt uncomfortable, but there was nothing vicious in Elena's questions. She was curious. He felt that. Believed it.

"I guess a woman just naturally explores a man more than a man does a woman. I know Laurie seemed always to know more about me, about my body, than I ever even thought about. She'd look at me in a funny way and then run her hands over my chest as if she knew there was a treasure inside. Like you're doing with me. It was mightly spooky sometimes."

"You loved her, didn't you?"

"I did. But she had more love in her than a man could handle. How can you give back so much love when you drown in it?"

"I know. You can't. But the worse thing is to give love and not get any back."

"Yes. That is bad. Women always seem to do that."

"What?"

"Give more love than they get back."

"How long ago did your. . . .did Laurie die?"

"Three years ago. A lifetime."

"How come no other woman caught your fancy?

Enough to marry I mean?"

"Laurie was special and I don't compare other gals to her. But she gave me a lot and it was hard to handle when she was alive. Hard after she died. I'm a drifter, Elena, pure and simple, and the sky means as much to me as the earth—and the earth means as much to me now as holding any woman. So I guess I'm like the other men you've known. No good, in a sense, but if so, then the land isn't any good either and no man who stands on it gives a damn about where he is or why."

Elena sucked in a breath, sighed.

"You do, Gunn. You give a damn."

She lay atop him, kissed him hard. Her hand grasped his cock, squeezed it. Her breasts flattened against the broadness of his chest. Her legs felt good, her body writhing against his with desire.

"Take me," she said, "before I get all choked up and cry my head off."

She rolled off him, spread her legs wide. Her breasts resumed their shape, the nipples taut as thumbs. He kissed each one, felt her body quiver. Her arms brought him to her and he dipped his hips, to spear her with his swollen probe. He sank into velvet fire, sliding through the smooth slick passage of her sex. To the deep cauldron of bubbling flesh. Fresh energy surged through him. Elena's body quickened. She thrust upwards, skewering his cock into her with an almost savage intensity. Her eyes went wild, her breath came hard, in short gasps as she matched his rhythms, urged him on with her thrashing body, her clamping quivering legs.

"Oh my!" she exclaimed. "It's—it's better than anything ever! Oh, go deep, Gunn, go deep. I—I'm coming like a geyser on the Yellowstone."

She bucked as the orgasm rippled through her.

Fingernails dug into his shoulders. She hung on as the spasm drove her body out of control. Hung on with sightless smokey eyes that filled with tears. Gunn waited, holding himself back, until his own excitement subsided.

Elena was passionate. Wanton. She clutched at him with a fearsome strength and he wondered how brutal Jersey Slim had been with her, how quick. There were fires in her that could not be quenched. He sensed that in her struggles, in the desperate look in her tear-filled eyes. Men had used her and misunderstood her probably. The Jersey Slims, the drifters like himself. But Elena was too good to be used up and tossed away like a broken flower. She was fire and flesh, the fluttering thunder of a woman's heartbeat in a man's ear, passionate and caring, tender and ferocious. A good woman.

"Oh, Gunn, I—I never came like that before. And you waited. You didn't come."

"No. Not yet."

"How? I—I didn't disappoint you, did I?"

"No."

"They—they usually come first. Before I do."

"Some men do, I reckon."

She slid her arms down his back, pinned his arms to his side. Squeezed him. She closed her eyes, took a deep breath. Held it. Quivered again. He pumped her slowly, sliding in and out of her steaming groove, brushing against the hard flesh of the clit-trigger. She opened her eyes. Looked at him with wonder. Her mouth opened as if she was going to say something, but she was silent. Looking into his eyes. Wondering. He smiled down at her. Sank deep until she shuddered. A long slow shudder that seemed endless, as if the earth itself was moving beneath her.

"You're very good to me," she said at last.

And the orgasm took her in its teeth, shook her as if she was a doll made of cast-off rags. Her eyes fluttered, the lids batting like shutters in a windstorm. Her face and neck turned strawberry, the veins swelling to blue rivulets under the surface of her skin. Her mouth opened in the abandonment of surrender and she rode out the tide, letting the lust of pleasure beat through her body like Apache drums.

Gunn marveled at the way her sex-cleft pressured him, expanding and contracting like a squeezing fist. Bringing him pleasure, too. A muscle in her loin throbbed like a charley horse. He felt it rattling against his inner thigh like a pulse beat out of control.

He rose up on straightened arms to see her, change the angle of his penetration. She looked small and vulnerable, her shoulders pressed against the bed, comely as anything he'd ever seen, the collar bones pushing against the tauntened skin so that she seemed made of delicate china. The strawberry color now bathed her shoulders, suffusing her flesh with a roseate glow.

To his surprise, she began banging her pelvic bone against his, thrusting upward with hearty lust, swaying her hips, grinding against him with powerful surges. Burying his shaft in the curly-haired nest, burying it deep in her love-channel. Deep in lava seas of foamy silk and hot froth. So deep he could almost feel the mouth of her womb open and pull at him with powerful suction.

He surrendered to her lust.

He let her impale herself on his throbbing bone and run with it like a mare with the bit in her teeth. Let her smash against him and tug him into her wallowing flesh as if to drown him in her hair, her breasts, her eyes, her joyous tears.

He pushed downward, letting her thrash and thrust, skewer and impale, his cock ramming against the hard bone and sinking into the wet hot depths of her pelvic cavity. He lost all track of time and place. The woman beneath him was lost, too. Lost in the throes of pleasure, the rapture of ecstasy.

The bedding roiled as Elena gave herself up to the spoils of sex with the tall man. It was all Gunn could do to keep up with her. Her orgasms were joltingly connected now until he could not tell where one left off and another began. She made little animal sounds in her throat and her fingernails became lethal, raking his shoulders and back every time she topped out from one of her spine-cracking climaxes. It was like riding a mustang before he was halter-broke. It was even more a thrill.

"I—I can't anymore—come now, Gunn," she gasped. "Do it before I go out of my mind."

Her body was sleek with sweat. Her hair was damp. Her breasts glistened in the shaded light, marvelously oiled mounds with jutting nipples.

Gunn gripped her buttocks, pulled her up against him. He rammed deep, pumped faster than he had before.

Elena screamed.

He jetted as she jangled with the frenzy of orgasm.

Boiled and exploded inside her as his brain raged with the pleasure of it. Her claws raked deep into his back, her legs kicked high, quivered.

Spent, he fell atop her, lay on her yielding breasts until his pulse rate subsided, until his heart stopped pounding in his chest. She relaxed her fingers, clasped him lovingly until he could hear her own heartbeat, the gentle puffs of breath as she regained her composure.

"God, you know a lot about women," she breathed. "More than any man I've ever known. You gave me so much."

Gunn was silent, locked away with his own thoughts.

"Where did you learn those things? Or did they just come natural?"

"A man learns from a woman," he said.

"You had good teachers."

He rolled off her body to let her breathe. He, too, was slick with sweat. It felt good. Another bath would put him just right. The dragging had not ruined anything important.

"Gunn? If you didn't kill Jersey Slim, he'll kill you. He couldn't stand to know this. That we had been together."

"Who's going to tell him?"

"He'll know. Even so, you bested him and he can't stand that either."

"I'll take that fork when I come to it."

"Yes," she said, "and it won't be long. Will you tell me what happened?"

"All of it?"

"Yes. Everything."

"I'll roll a smoke."

He told her all that had happened, with Santos, Pepe, and Jersey Slim. She listened raptly, her eyes flickering at certain points. When he was finished, she sat up, a look of fear on her face.

"Santos!" she spat. "He'll be back here. Looking for that woman, Eva Morgan. And Junia's out there. He—he'll find her, use her to get back in the good graces of Enriquez. You've got to find her, Gunn! She's in danger!"

Gunn realized that Elena was probably right. Junia had been gone a long time. If Santos got to Eva. . . .

"I'll go now," he said, rising from the bed. "Can you handle yourself if Santos comes here?"

Elena nodded, shooing him away.

Gunn looked down at the floor, at the pile of Elena's clothes. A long slim dagger lay on top, deadly in its garter scabbard.

Yes, Elena could handle herself.

He was glad she was on his side.

FIFTEEN

Pedro Santos watched as Junia Diaz came out of the hotel, looked both ways, then walked primly down the street. Her skirt swayed with the rhythm of her hips. His mind worked quickly with the new information.

Gunn had worn a thunderbird that had belonged to Elena Sutter.

Now, Junia Diaz was in town.

At the same hotel where Gunn was staying.

That meant Elena was probably there too. Now. With Gunn. And the Morgan girl as well.

Santos smiled, came out of the shadows between the buildings where he had been waiting, trying to make up his mind about his next move. It was all very clear now.

He began to follow Junia, quickening his pace to catch up with her without appearing to be after her. He didn't know who was looking, but he didn't want to be too obvious. The meeting must look as if it had come about by chance. He didn't want Junia screaming her head off in broad daylight. Some people might get the wrong idea and go after him. Because Junia, for whatever else she was, was a woman.

Junia didn't seem in any particular hurry. Nor did she behave as if she was afraid. Yet she was going somewhere.

Where?

Santos lagged back as Junia looked in windows, crossed the street once, then returned to his side. Shopping? Perhaps. She carried a small carpetbag, but as far as he knew, she had never had much money. Like the other women in camp, she was a piece of chattel, little better than a slave.

Santos turned his face once when Junia stopped at a store window, peered through the sunshot pane. She didn't look in his direction, but seemed absorbed by whatever was in the window. When he turned back, she was gone. His heart sank until he realized that she had gone inside the shop. He crossed the street, looked over at the store.

Lucy's Dress Shoppe.

Santos snorted. Lucy was Lucinda Gomez and she copied mail order catalogs for the dresses she sold. He knew her. She wanted to be a fancy lady, but she had been a whore in Juarez before she had come to Tres Piedras. In the window were dressmaker's dummies sporting fancy dresses. Junia would look like a whore in either one of them. And that's what she was as far as Santos was concerned.

He had little regard for women. Born in Sonora, Santos grew up poor, remembering with horror his own swollen belly like those of his brothers, sisters and friends. They lived on corn and beans, little meat. Once he had killed a chicken that belonged to a neighbor and his mother had looked on stupidly while

167

the man caned him half to death. Yet that night they had eaten fresh meat. Not once had his mother thanked him for the extra food. In fact, she had clucked about his sinful ways and warned him that he would perish in hell if he turned out to be a thief.

Yet Santos soon learned that thieves were the only ones who did not have the swollen bellies and who had money in their pockets. His father was a *peon* and worked long hard hours on land that belonged to rich people. When Pedro was old enough he was expected to work on the same land, help with the household finances, meagre as they were. He went to the huge *rancho* one morning and saw the rich fields, the fat beeves, the beautiful horses and his eyes glittered like star-struck gems. It was difficult for him to believe that people lived that way, while those who worked to make the cattle fat, the horses sleek, the fields green and fruitful, grubbed like dogs for scraps of meat and parched corn to fill their empty and aching bellies.

He had turned thief and killed his first man.

Stealing a few head of cattle, at first, he moved on the horses. All from the vast Huerta *rancho*. He soon learned where to take the stock, how to alter brands, whom to trust. No one.

He killed the foreman on the *rancho* and took to the owlhoot trail, moving up through Mexico and into the borderlands.

And things were not so good until he met Enriquez.

Since then, he had lived well. Even with the soldiers dogging them, he lived better than any of his family in Mexico. Better than most men on the wrong side of the law.

Now, he was about to lose all that.

Unless Gunn had killed Jersey Slim Norris.

Junia would know. She had seen Gunn.

Santos waited across the street from Lucy's, a warm feeling beginning to build in his stomach.

Junia was in the shop for only a few minutes. She did not come out with a package as Santos expected. Instead, she started across the street to the dry goods store, passing a couple on the way, smiling at them.

Santos hurried to intercept her.

Junia did not see him coming. As she reached the entrance to B. Hidalgo's Dry Goods Store, a hand closed on her wrist.

She gasped, turned. Stared into Santos' smiling face.

"Good morning," he said amiably in Spanish. "Do not yell or I'll gut you where you stand. Smile and come with me if you do not want trouble, eh?"

"Santos! *Cabron!*"

"Now, don't curse me, woman. Just walk along with me if you do not want your wrist broken."

His grip tightened.

Junia got the message.

Her face drained of blood, but she allowed Santos to push her along the street, guiding her while he smiled and talked nonsense. She was frozen with fear, her eyes pleading with passersby who ignored the couple.

"Turn down here," Santos said tightly, shoving on her elbow. They took a side street that would lead them away from the foot traffic, out back of the false fronts of the main street. Santos hurried her along as soon as they passed the last building. A prairie dog, standing on hind legs, shrieked a warning. There was a scurry of animals diving into holes.

Santos looked over his shoulder.

No one was following them.

He headed toward a pile of rocks that would offer concealment.

Junia saw where they were going and began to resist, balk. She halted, her saddles scuffing the dirt. She twisted free of Pedro's grasp.

"What are you doing?" she asked. "I do not want to go with you, Santos!"

"Keep still, woman. I am just taking you to a place where we can talk private. There are some questions you can answer."

"I won't." She glared at him with mock defiance. Her eyes told him that she was frightened. She looked wildly around for help. There was no one to come to her assistance. The soft breeze blew against the rocks, hummed in the saguaros. They might as well have been miles from a town. Only the barren backs of buildings showed that there were any people and none of them were visible. Horses nickered in the corrrals behind the livery. Otherwise, it was quiet.

"You will," he said, reaching out for her.

His hand touched her arm. She snatched it away as if burned by his fingers.

Santos stepped up a pace and slapped her face. Hard.

Junia cried out, but her voice did not carry. Scowling, Santos clapped a hand over her mouth, an arm around her waist. He dragged her, kicking and moaning through his hand, toward the rocks. He shoved her behind them, out of sight. She cowered in shadow.

"D—don't hurt me," she whimpered.

"I ought to cut you bad," he puffed. "You're a little

170

troublemaker, woman, but you will do what I say. If you want to keep what's left of your face."

Santos stood over her, feeling tall. He had never had Junia, but he could have. She was just a tramp. They had picked her up in a raid on a small pueblo near the Texas-Mexican border. He couldn't even remember the name of the settlement. Two, maybe three years ago. She couldn't have been more than fourteen or fifteen then. She was still only a girl. But she had blossomed and grown. It gave him a sense of power to have her fear him.

"What do you want to know?" she asked when he hadn't said anything for several seconds. She backed against the rocks, pressing her buttocks on them for security.

Santos cracked a dry laugh.

"That's better, little Junia. If you are nice, I will not hurt you, understand?"

Junia nodded eagerly.

"I want to know about Gunn," he said.

"I know nothing. It is true. Nothing."

Santos' smile vanished.

His face darkened like a thundercloud.

He lashed out, slapped her again. This time, Junia did not cry out. Tears stuggled to fill her eyes, but she bit her lip defiantly. Trying not to show how terrified she was to be alone with this man.

Santos grabbed her handbag, jerked it from her grip.

She gasped, tried to get it back.

"Don't move!" Santos snarled.

He opened the carpetbag, looked inside. Saw the money. He drew out the bills.

"What have we here? Money? Where did you get all this money, Junia? It is not your money. Gunn must have given it to you. Or did you steal it from Paco?"

"It—it's not Paco's," she said, confused.

"No. It is not yours either." He acted as if he was going to pocket the money. Junia grabbed for it. Santos bent backwards, holding the wad of bills just out of her reach.

"Who gave you this money? Gunn?"

Junia's eyes took on a feral look of cunning. Santos moved closer, holding the money Gunn had given her in front of her. His other hand moved slightly and Junia saw that he was reaching for a knife. Her eyes shifted back to his. She let out a long sigh.

"Yes. Gunn gave me the money. It is for clothes. He is bad hurt. His clothes are all torn and dirty."

"Aha!" gloated Santos. "So, did he tell you about the fight?"

Junia shook her head.

"You lie!"

Santos let the money fall to the ground. He drew his knife.

"No!" screamed Junia. "It—it was with Jersey Slim! There was a bad fight."

Santos licked his lips. His hand froze. As long as Junia talked she was in no danger. She knew that. But she also knew that she didn't know all the answers. She had seen Gunn only briefly and did not know all that had happened. If Santos thought she was lying he would cut her. She shuddered.

"Did he kill Slim?"

"I don't know. He did not talk about it with me. Or with Elena. He just gave me the money and said he needed clothes."

"He was there a long time. You could have talked with him."

"He was bathing. I saw him for only a few moments. Please, you must believe me."

Santos considered what Junia had told him. She could be telling the truth. Gunn may not have told her what had happened. Perhaps he told Elena. But he could not go there now. Gunn was still there. He had probably sent Junia away on purpose so that he could lift the skirts of Slim's girlfriend. But Junia knew other things. Things of value.

"All right," he smiled, sheathing his knife. "I believe you, woman. Gunn did not talk to you of Slim. Do you think he killed Norris?"

Junia shrugged, relieved that Santos had put away the knife.

"I think so. Elena gave him a pretty necklace with a thunderbird of silver and turquoise. I think that Slim must have been pretty mad if he saw this Gunn wearing that around his neck. I think he would want to kill Gunn. There must have been a terrible fight. I saw Gunn's body. It was all marked and scratched with bruises and cuts. So, he must have killed Slim."

"Yes. That is true. He must have. Let us be friends. I mean you no harm. It is just that I do not like lying. We can get along, you and I. Eh?"

"Clearly, we can. It is only that I must get the clothes for the *Señor* Gunn. He is naked and has nothing to wear but a wet towel.

Santos threw his head back and laughed.

"Oh, I think he will wear the little fur piece between the legs of Elena for a little while, Junia. No?"

Junia's face darkened as she flushed with embarrassment.

"Oh, yes, Junia. He might wear it on his face for a while and then. . . ."

"Stop it! Do not joke so!"

The bandit's face hardened as he realized that his own cruelty was making himself uncomfortable. He did not want to think of Gunn and Slim's woman. He did not want Junia to think he was preoccupied with such thoughts. After all, he could find his own women. He did not have to worry about those with other men.

"And you, Junia, you have run away from our band? From Enriquez? For good?"

"Yes," she pouted.

"Where will you go? What will you do?"

"I will go with Elena. We will ride far away and find a good life where men are decent to us."

Santos suppressed the urge to laugh. To humiliate Junia with her past, her chances for a future. After all, in this western country even a humble woman could make something of herself. Could erase the past like sandmarks in a windstorm. Like Lucinda with her dress shop.

"Come," he said, "let us go back to town and be friends. I will buy you a drink for your trouble, some sweets if you wish.

Junia was suspicious.

"No, I cannot do that. I should not be seen on the street much. Someone may be looking for me. Are you not with Enriquez anymore?"

"That depends. If. . . ." But Santos did not want to tell this girl what was on his mind. He had started to say that if Slim was dead then he could go back and join the band without anyone being the wiser. If Slim was alive, then he could not go back. Not without proving himself all over again. To Enriquez and to Jersey Slim. It would not be easy.

"Are you or are you not?"

He saw the flicker of fear in her eyes again. He stepped away from her to calm her down. He needed to ask her one more thing and then he would be through with her. It was not his intention to harm her much, anyway. He still needed Gunn. But, just as much, he needed the woman, Eva Morgan. He could see Enriquez' eyes light up when he saw a new woman in camp, one brought especially to him. Enriquez was *macho*, but he had not time to play games with females. He had them brought to him, like the offerings of serfs to landowners, and he toyed with them as he wished. That was the way he, Pedro, would like to be one day. The *patron*, the man people respected and looked up to.

The Morgan girl could make him a big man with Enriquez. Fresh meat in camp. And, if he brought back Junia, that would help, too.

Santos speculated now with a kind of animal cunning.

If he had the Morgan girl, Gunn would surely follow him to the camp, try to free her and her father. That would be just as good as bringing him there. It was so simple. Why had he not thought of it before? Because he didn't have Junia to help him.

"Where is this Eva Morgan?" he asked Junia suddenly.

Startled, she bit her lip.

"Why—why do you want to know?"

"Curiosity."

"I—I don't know where she is. Gunn took her away somewhere. He—he hid her someplace."

Junia was not a convincing liar. Santos didn't believe her.

"*Mentirosa!*" he snapped. "I'm warning you, Junia, I will not be soft with you. I need to talk to the Morgan woman and you know where she is."

"No—no, I can't tell you," she blurted. "Gunn—he asked me not to."

"She is with Gunn?"

Junia shook her head.

"Is she in Tres Piedras?"

Junia nodded.

Santos grinned. He was getting somewhere. And it was even better than he had expected. Eva Morgan was not with Gunn. She was hiding somewhere. He'd bet a hundred pesos Junia knew where she was too!

"Well, why don't we go and talk to her," said Santos.

"No. I must get back to Gunn, give him some clothes."

Santos' apparent amiability vanished. He reached out, grabbed Junia by the throat. Squeezed. She tried to scream, but could make no sign. Her lips started to turn gray.

"Tell me where the woman is or I'll crush your throat," Santos rasped. Panic in her eyes, Junia nodded. The bandit relaxed his grip. Junia was on her knees, gasping for breath, choking. He nudged her with his boot. "Hurry, Junia or it will not be so pleasant for you."

"Honora. She's at Honora Bienvenidos. But she is

hurt. Paco shot her."

"Come. You will go there with me. If you are lying. . . ."

"I'm not lying! The woman is there!"

Santos didn't listen. He pulled Junia after him as he headed toward the back entrance of the livery stable. He knew where Honora lived. He had once made her daughter pregnant. Little Ofelia had been fourteen. She died in childbirth. Honora hated him and he hated her. It wasn't his fault her daughter had been weak. He owed her nothing, but she had better not stand in his way. He meant to deliver Eva Morgan to Enriquez.

Wounded or sound.

Dead or alive.

SIXTEEN

Enriquez bobbed in the saddle, his back straight, his paunch bulging over his gunbelt. Behind him, swarthy men followed by twos, their horses laden with booty. Further back came the wagons, three small ones, bouncing along with wood creaking, leather whining. The mules protested, but flankers kept them moving with quirts and lusty, low cries.

Enriquez looked again at the Freund Sharps across his pommel. It gleamed in the sun.

"You like the new rifles, Umberto?"

"*Sí, patron.* They are very fine." Umberto Peña rubbed a hand over the stock of his new Sharps. "They speak with a strong voice."

"The raid was good, I think. The first. Taos will never miss a few people this year. But the goods will go there to the fair and we will make our profit, thanks to the unwilling generosity of a few."

Umberto laughed at his *jefe's* joke. Many of the goods they now had on the wagons would still wind up at the Taos Fair, but they would be altered, remarked, and sold by various members of the gang for 100%

profit. The morning raid had gone smoothly and swiftly, even without Jersey Slim along. The scouts had come in to camp before dawn, told of seeing the wagon encampment half day's ride. Enriquez had been angry that Slim was gone and the two girls, but he had mounted the raiding expedition himself and now was swelling with pride. They had killed two drivers, taken a white girl prisoner. The wagons carried tools, branding irons, cooking utensils and wool blankets. The wool blankets were rare prizes and would bring good prices.

"You did well, *mi jefe*," said Umberto. "And there will be more wagons in the days to come."

"Yes, the scouts did a fine job. There is a large train from Sante Fe due to arrive at the mountain pass in two days. By then, perhaps, we will know what became of Jersey Slim and those bad runaway girls."

"And what of Pedro Santos?" asked Umberto.

"Ah, poor Santos. He tries hard, but he does not always succeed. If he does not bring Gunn and the Morgan girl tonight, we will go looking for him."

"Maybe this Gunn had shot him too."

"Maybe," said Enriquez, refusing to spoil his good mood with bad thoughts. He squinted up into the sun. They would make the canyon camp in another hour. The men were all in good spirits, the wagons were moving well. A few clouds banked the southern horizon but the sky over them was clear. A buzzard circled in the distance and, as he watched, was joined by another. That could mean something, but he was not sure. Still, it was good to stay alert. No one was following them, but someone could be up ahead.

Enriquez lifted a hand.

The column came to a halt.

"Umberto," he said, "send a couple of men to scout ahead. Two more should go over the tracks again, brush them out for a mile or so back."

"Ay, but yes. I will send Alonzo Calderon to scout. You see the buzzards, as well. It could be nothing, but they are circling lower. It could mean they have spotted the carrion."

Even as they watched, more buzzards appeared out of nowhere, joining the first two on the invisible spiral until the air seemed filled with the big birds, all swirling around in a vast airy chimney.

"Calderon!" Umberto called. *Ven pá 'ca!*

Umberto issued the orders to the young lean bandit, watched him ride toward the circling buzzards. Then he rode back to set men to sweep the trail free of tracks with cut brush. Since the raid, they had done this to avoid pursuit. The efforts would not fool an expert tracker, but the people they preyed upon were largely merchants, traders, artisans. Most of them would just turn around and go back from whence they had come and the others would complain and try to hire on in Taos until they could earn enough money to return to their homes and shops.

Enriquez waited until Umberto returned.

Then, he raised his hand, pushed the palm forward through the air.

"Onward!" he said. The wagons and horses jerked into motion. More and more buzzards drifted into the swirling flock ahead until there were at least two dozen.

Umberto could almost smell the death the buzzards smelled.

180

He did not like it. The place was too near the hideout where a skeleton crew of guards watched over the camp and the gunsmith, Ethan Morgan. He did not express his fears to Enriquez, however. If Enriquez was worried, it was up to him, as chief, to say something. He would not appreciate one of his men speaking of trouble. Superstition was a powerful force among these men.

Unconsciously, Enriquez picked up the pace until a cloud of dust rose in the still dry air. Umberto looked over his shoulder nervously, but did not dare to mention that they were leaving a better trail than the one in the dirt. Anyone looking for them could track them by the spool of dust that began to string out and hang like tell-tale smoke over the saguaros. The wagons followed the chief's lead and that was that.

A quarter hour of riding and clouds on the far horizon had spread out, thickened like whey-curds, pushed by a breeze hundreds of miles to the south, perhaps arising out of the Gulf of Mexico itself.

But Enriquez wasn't looking at the clouds.

The buzzards grew larger and more numerous. Yet none had descended to the earth as yet. Instead, a pair flew low and the others hovered effortlessly above as if wired there to orbit silently. Waiting. Waiting for something or someone to die.

But who?

His stomach growled with worry.

Enriquez thought of the camp and his prisoner. Perhaps someone had come and killed them all. Soldiers? His scouts had reported no army activity to him. Of course a small band of well-trained troops could slip past his scouts. If they knew exactly where to go. Only a few people could tell them. That bitch whore Elena Sutter. Junia Diaz. Pedro Santos.

Jersey Slim Norris.

But Jersey Slim would not do such a thing. Enriquez trusted him. The man was a *gringo*, but he was sour on other *gringos*. He was loyal. He had proved himself in battle after battle, raid after raid.

No, not Jersey Slim.

Not even Santos. He was an outlaw by choice. He would not betray them.

The women, though, had proved their disloyalty by running away. Slim would take care of them. Indeed, it was almost certain that is why he left without saying anything. He had tracked them. Maybe he had killed them in a particularly horrible way. Staked them out for tarantulas, the snakes and the scorpions. The ants. Slim would do such a thing. Out of anger. A deep hatred that was a thing to admire. Enriquez knew about that hatred. He had seen it work in Slim, seen it twist his twisted face into even more horrible shape than it already was.

Enriquez threw up his hand suddenly, pulled off the trail.

Now he did.

Umberto almost ran into him, even so. He had been looking over his shoulder and did not see what the chief had seen.

Riding towards them, fast, was Calderon. Whipping his horse and jabbing his big-rowled spurs into the flanks of the animal. The horse's mane flared in the speed-created breeze.

Umberto uttered an oath.

"Something has frightened him," observed Enriquez, as the wagon brakes screeched, leather groaned. The dust cloud stopped at that point, but Calderon's horse was spooling out a cloud of its own, galloping with nostrils distended, neck outstretched. Calderon reined him expertly through the cactus, twisting in the saddle with every twist and turn so as not to be unseated. It was deadly country to take a fall in, with cactus, snakes and the dreaded Gila all waiting for the luckless rider who did such a thing.

"He is very afraid, I think," agreed Umberto, his horse sidling away from the trail rump-first. "I have never seen him ride so fast."

Enriquez drew his rifle from its scabbard.

"Someone could be chasing him," the leader said.

Umberto drew his rifle. There was the swick of metal slithering out of leather holsters and sheaths, the metallic click of hammers being cocked as the other bandits in the rear, who were encased in a cloud of dust and could not see, followed Umberto's and their chief's lead.

Calderon reined up, skidding his horse. The animal was lathered, chest heaving. Wind rattled in rales through its chest.

"*Mi jefe,*" Calderon blurted, "I have just seen a terrible thing. Most terrible. I do not know what to make of it. You must all come quick!"

"What are you saying, Calderon?" asked Enriquez, his face clouding with a mixture of apprehension and anger. "Is someone chasing you? Have the soldiers come?"

"No, no!" panted the out-of-breath Calderon, "it is a dead man and Jersey Slim Norris. They are together and maybe Slim is dead too."

Enriquez rode closer, his curiosity bristling.

"Do not babble, man!" he said, a dangerous lilt to his voice. "What is this about Jersey Slim?"

"Where the buzzards are. . . .he is down, raving, insane. There is a dead man tied to his back. And Slim has the purple tongue, the red eyes. His face is a hideous sight to behold. I was scared. I ran to get someone. He—he did not see me. He is cursing a man. A man I did not see."

"What is the man's name?" asked Enriquez, leaning forward in the saddle, gripping the Sharps so tight his knuckles were white.

"Gunn."

★   ★   ★

The three men rode up, looked at the place where Calderon pointed.

"It was there I saw him."

No one was there.

Enriquez was about to backhand the scout for lying when they all heard a groan. Umberto wheeled his horse, rode to a small rise. He turned to say something and then leaned over, regurgitated.

Enriquez scowled.

Calderon started to get sick, gulped in air.

"What is it? Do you see something? What is the matter with you two? Are you women?"

"It is Slim," gasped Umberto, and crossed himself. *"Dios mio.* Never have I seen anything like it."

Enriquez rode up alongside Umberto. He looked down the slope, saw what had made his men sick. The chief's jaw turned to iron though and he did not wince.

Instead, his eyes narrowed and something boiled in his gut.

"Enriquez!" shrieked Jersey Slim and his voice turned the blood of those who watched to an icy chill.

Jersey Slim staggered toward Enriquez, his face a mask of blood and dirt, his body bristling with cactus spines, his clothes shredded. His hands were tied behind his back with the same rope that held the dead man over his shoulders. The dead man had bloated in the sun. His swollen face jutted next to Slim's, the eyes black. Except there were no eyes. The sockets had been picked clean by buzzards.

"Cut him loose!" Enriquez said to Umberto.

Umberto sat there, frozen in horror.

Enriquez reached over, pulled Umberto's knife from its scabbard. He dismounted, stalked down to where Slim stood, swaying. The man on his back was ripe. The stench was unbearable. Enriquez sawed through the ropes. The dead body slipped down. Slim stepped out of his bonds, rubbed his raw wrists gingerly.

"Who is that?" Enriquez asked, turning away from the sickening stench.

"A townie that got in the way," Slim croaked. He stank of death and decaying flesh. "Name of Pepe. I killed him."

"Who did this to you?"

"Gunn, who else? The bastard. I'm going to deball that sombitch and feed his gizzard to the wolves."

Slim began jerking cactus spines from his flesh. Blod oozed from the holes. He never flinched. His bad eye leaked over his torn face, but he seemed oblivious to his appearance. Enriquez stepped away, stood upwind.

Calderon rode up to the top of the knoll, his stomach fluttering. Enriquez saw him there, hailed him.

"Get off your horse, Alonzo! You ride with Umberto. Slim, can you ride?"

"You're fuckin' A-John I can ride!" He pulled a cactus needle out of one buttock. "I'm goin' after that son."

"Do not be in too much a hurry, *mi amigo,*" soothed the bandit leader. "There is much to talk about. We missed you on the raid this morning. You will need some salve and a bath, fresh clothes. Ride Calderon's horse to the camp with us and we will talk about what should be done."

"Just so's I get to tack that motherhumper's hide to the wall," Slim grumbled. He sagged and Enriquez thought he was going to fall. But he stood up on creaky legs, a piteous sight. His anger made him strong and he started walking toward Calderon's horse. Calderon gave him a wide berth as he walked to where Umberto waited.

"You'll get your revenge, Slim," said Enriquez. "I promise you that."

★　　★　　★

Santos ordered three horses saddled at the livery.

Juan Cardona knew better than to argue with Santos. He knew the man was a bandit. Like everyone else in Tres Piedras, he knew who he rode with: Enriquez.

Junia started to say something a couple of times, but a sharp look from Santos made her keep her mouth shut each time.

"You ride the small chestnut," he told her. "Lead the other one. Do not let it loose."

"Who is going to pay for these horses?" asked Cardona meekly.

"You will be paid. Meanwhile, just be happy that you are alive and that you will eat with your old woman tonight."

Santos rode his own horse, a wiry grulla. Junia held the reins of a sorry bay with a moth-eaten saddle on its back. It would have to do.

They rode out back of the livery, took the street leading to Honora Bienvenidos' house. Santos looked over his shoulder more than once, scanned the adobes and sod shacks they passed. The smell of fresh ground corn and tortillas cooking on round ovens assailed their nostrils, made them hungry. No one paid them any attention beyond a few curious children playing in the dirty street.

Honora lived in an adobe near the end.

Santos saw no horses tied to the rickety hitch-rail out front. He smiled with faint satisfaction.

"Are you sure the Morgan girl is here?" he asked Junia.

"Yes. I am not lying to you."

"We will ride around the house, come in from the back. If you see Gunn, you let me know. I do not want any surprises."

Junia was silent, but she started looking for Gunn. Hoping that she would see him.

They rode on past Honora's house. Santos did not look at it directly, but peered out of the corner of his eye to see if anyone was watching. He saw nothing suspicious. At the end of the street, he turned right, went down the narrow alley. He made Junia ride in front. He looked at the back of Honora's adobe, saw clothing hanging on thin rope lines, smoke coming from a small chimney that was a hole high in the back wall. He knew the inside wall, but it had been a long time since he had been there. He could almost smell the medicines and antiseptics that Honora kept in there. It always made him a little sick to his stomach.

"Keep on going," Santos said when Junia looked back at him.

They rode on past the adobe.

"That's far enough," he said, when they were out of sight of Honora's. "Stop."

Junia halted, waited for him. Santos stood up in the stirrups, looked back. He waited five minutes. No one had followed them. No one had come out of Honora's to see about them. The other adobes were quiet. People were asleep in the heat of the day, or eating.

"Get off. We'll tie the horses to that rail over there." Someone had built a crude fence for hogs. There were no hogs in the pen. Santos secured the reins of his horse and the one for Eva Morgan. He checked Junia's to see if she was trying to pull any tricks. Her reins were tied tightly.

"Walk in front of me. When we get to her door, you knock. I will be standing to your side, out of sight. Ask if you can see the Morgan girl. When you go in, I'll be right behind you."

"Don't hurt Honora, please!"

"Shut your mouth!"

At the door, Junia knocked quietly.

"Louder!" Santos whispered.

Honora opened the door.

"Junia! What are you doing back here?"

"I—I came to see Eva," she stuttered.

"But you should have come in the front. You don't have to. . . ."

Santos didn't wait.

He drew his pistol, shoved Junia into Honora.

"Hello, *Señora* Bienvenidos," he said tersely. "I have come to see your patient, Eva Morgan."

Honora didn't scream. She didn't even register surprise. She looked at Santos with a cold hatred limning her eyes.

"Leave her alone!" she said.

"Where is she? In the sick room?" Santos kicked the door shut.

"She is sleeping."

"Get out of my way," he warned, brandishing his pistol.

Honora stepped aside. Santos bulled past her and Junia, went to the first door down the hall. He listened for a minute, heard breathing. He opened the door.

There was a hulk under the covers on the bed.

Santos blinked. The mound was much too big for a girl. It took him a minute to realize that something was wrong.

Before he could cock his pistol, the covers moved and a figure rose up.

Santos stared into the barrel of a Colt .45.

"You!" he breathed, his knees turning to jelly.

SEVENTEEN

"Just let it down slow," said Gunn. "Move that thumb and I'll blow your hand off at the wrist."

Santos moved his arm, letting it sink. His thumb remained frozen over the hammer of his pistol.

"Put it on the floor and step toward me," Gunn said, swinging his legs over the side of the bed.

Santos did as he was told.

Gunn touched the floor with his boots, stood up. He towered over Santos.

"Are you going to shoot me?"

"I might," said Gunn. "You deserve it."

Santos looked at the *gringo*, saw the ugly welts on his face, the scratches. He had been in some kind of fight. His clothes were ripped and patches of purple flesh showed through. It was as he had looked riding into town, but close up he looked even worse.

"You still need me," said Santos.

"Maybe."

"Did you kill Norris?"

"Why, Santos? He a friend of yours?"

"I know him. He is the *segundo* for Enriquez."

"He won't be much use to Enriquez for a while."

"Then you didn't kill him."

"No. Back on out of here, real slow." Gunn reached down and picked up Santos' pistol. In the hall, he prodded the Mexican toward the front room. The two women followed behind Gunn.

Gunn couldn't be sure, but when he had told Santos that Jersey Slim was still alive, he had seen a change in Santos' expression. A crestfallen look. Slight, but there. Maybe he could use that information to his advantage.

"Sit," Gunn ordered when they reached the livingroom. Santos found a chair. A chair he had known well—once. Honora and Junia sat meekly together on the worn divan. Gunn shoved Santos' pistol inside his waistband and remained standing.

He didn't say anything, but watched as Santos began to squirm. The women, too, fixed the Mexican bandit with accusing stares. It was an effective method of torture. Santos was guilty of deceit and treachery. Maybe more. Gunn had already heard about Honora's daughter. He didn't give much of a damn for a man who treated women that way. He shuddered to think of Eva, or Junia for that matter, in the hands of a man like Santos.

"You are a smart man, Gunn," Santos said finally. Sweat broke out on his forehead, soaked into the sweatband of his hat, dripped into his eyebrows. "I did not think you would come here."

"It wasn't hard to figure, Santos. You've been playing a mighty wild game with me. I don't trust you. You got at least one man killed and I figure you to doublecross anybody sitting at the same table with you."

191

"You need me," said Santos, a faint tinge of pleading in his voice. "I can get you in Enriquez's camp. That still goes. I was going to do that this morning when you and Pepe came out to the *jacal.*"

"Maybe. Go on, Santos."

"Tonight we can go there. We can go in quietly. I know the guards. They will pass me through."

The two women exchanged glances.

"Do not trust this man," said Honora quietly.

"That was the plan anyway, wasn't it Santos?" Gunn asked. "Only Enriquez figured to dry-gulch me once I got in."

Gunn watched the man's sweaty bronze face for a sign of fishtailing. Santos blinked, swallowed. He looked at the pistol in Gunn's hand. Licked dry lips.

"Yes," he said. "That was the plan."

Gunn smiled coldly.

"Here's the way it's going to be, Santos. Listen real close." Gunn walked to the front door, leaned against it. "I'm going to let you go now. Ride back into town or on back to your bandit bunch. Makes no never mind to me. But if you're not in the lobby of the hotel before dusk, waiting for me, I'll come gunning for you as soon as this is over. I give you your choice. If you do run out on me or try another trick, I'll sure as hell come after you—and it won't be just for palaver. Savvy?"

Santos nodded.

"Way I figure it, you and Jersey Slim are on the outs. He'll kill you if you go back there without me. And I reckon you wanted to take the Morgan gal back to Enriquez. Put yourself in his graces. That won't work. I'm going to give your pistol to Honora here and she'll kill you dead if you ever step back inside her home. That right, Honora?"

Honora nodded somberly.

Gunn walked over, slipped Santos' gun out of his waistband, handed it to Honora, butt-first. She aimed it at Santos, cocked it. Her hand didn't waver.

Santos swallowed again.

"I would love to shoot you, Pedro Santos," said Honora.

"Remember, Santos. At the hotel, before dusk. Unarmed." Gunn turned to Junia. "I'll be with you in a minute. We'll go get me some duds and go back to the hotel together. I imagine Elena's right anxious to see you're all right."

"*Gracias, señor,*" breathed Junia.

Gunn holstered his pistol, walked back down the hall. He entered Honora's bedroom, saw Eva Morgan lying on the bed, chalk-faced, her eyes wide.

"Oh, thank goodness. I heard the voices and then it was quiet. What's going on?"

Gunn sat next to her on the bed. He put his hand on hers. She turned it over, squeezed his hand in hers.

"I'll explain it all later. Or, Honora can tell you about it. The main thing is that you're going to be O.K. I'm going after your father tonight, Eva. I think I stand a pretty good chance of getting in, throwing some confusion into that bunch and getting out alive. Don't worry."

"I will worry," she said.

"You feeling any better?"

"Now that you're here," she said softly. "I wish you could stay."

"I wish I could too."

He leaned over, kissed her gently. She put her arms around him, winced as her wound was stretched. She kissed him hard, ignored the pain. Honora was a good nurse. She had cleaned and packed the wound, packed it with healing unguents, bandaged it. She had given her some powders for her fever. Gunn had come to the house, arranged for her to be moved to Honora's bedroom while he took her place on the sick bed. He hadn't explained much, but evidently his plan had worked. She sighed deeply, grateful that he was alive and with her.

"Goodbye, Eva," he said, pulling away from her. "I'll see you real soon."

"Hurry back safely," she said.

Gunn closed the door quietly behind him.

"Come on, Santos," Gunn said, "we might just as well use those horses you brought out here."

Santos' eyes flickered.

"Oh, we saw you go by and circle the house. I walked over here." To Honora, he said: "Keep your eyes peeled. Is there anybody in this town who will ride with me or help you out?"

Honora shook her head, dipped her eyelashes sadly.

"I figured not. *Ten cuidado, Señora.*"

"*Si. Usted tambien. Vaya con Dios.*"

★ ★ ★

Gunn and Junia left Santos at the livery stable, walked down the street to do their shopping.

"Do you think he will be there as you asked?" Junia looked back over her shoulder as if expecting Santos to run away.

194

Gunn shrugged.

"I'll go without him, if he's not. Come one. I need clothes and a few more things to take with me tonight. You want to go back to the hotel first?"

"No, I will go with you. I am very frightened of Santos."

"Elena can take care of herself. I told her he might go to my room or to Honora's. She'll not let anyone in the room until we get back."

Gunn bought clothes for himself, dresses for the two girls. He then went to the hardware store and bought some other items, carried them over his shoulder in a gunny sack. Junia carried the bundle of clothes. It was past noon and Gunn stopped in at La Paloma restaurant and ordered three meals sent up to the hotel room in half an hour. He ordered beef, beans, tortillas and *chili verde* with rice brought in earthen containers to keep them hot.

Back at the hotel, he knocked four times on his door.

"Gunn?"

"Yes, Elena. Junia and I are here."

Elena was overjoyed to see them. Her face lit up like an Arizona sunrise as the two swept into the room. Gunn closed and locked the door.

"Elena, Junia," he said quickly, "we haven't much time. I want you to tell me everything you know about Enriquez, his men, the layout of the camp, the weapons, anything you can think of."

"But we alread. . . ."

"Again," he insisted. "Every bit of it. Santos may take me there tonight, but he may not. I want to know everything I can before I go out there—with or without him."

Gunn listened carefully, asked questions. The food arrived and they ate. Still, the girls talked. They told him about the personal habits of each bandit. They told him of Enriquez, of how he sent out scouts, the routines he established for the guards, which varied weekly, if not daily, his behavior on raids, how he treated his men, which foods he preferred (hated pork, loved chicken), who was a light sleeper, who wasn't. He learned of the guards at the box canyon entrance, how many and where they usually sat or stood. Some of it he had heard before, but much of it was new.

At two that afternoon, the stragglers and survivors of that morning's raid arrived in town. Gunn heard the commotion, went down to see what all the fuss was about. He stayed long enough to learn that the merchants had been attacked by bandits. It didn't take any deep figuring to know who the bandits were. This information was valuable too. He returned to the hotel room, ready to sleep, rest, before meeting Santos late in the afternoon. If he showed.

"I have learned a lot," he told Junia and Elena. "With your help, I think I can do what I have to do. Now, there has been a raid. It couldn't be more perfect. From what you've told me, Enriquez will celebrate tonight. He and his men will get blind drunk."

"Not all of them," Elena reminded him.

"No. He'll double or triple the guards. You told me that. Thanks. But two other factors give me hope. One, I know where he keeps the ammunition for the rifles and pistols. If I can isolate that, I have a chance. Two, Jersey Slim, if he made it, will have gotten back by now, or soon. A lot of the men will wonder about him. How he got beat and put to shame by a *gringo*. Those men will have fear as their enemy. One look at me, or knowing I'm in camp, should put them off stride, on edge. I'll beat him. Morgan will help, too, once he knows I'm there. He's a pretty strong and determined character."

"You're right," said Elena thoughtfully, "many of the *bandidos* are superstitious. They will be afraid if they know you have come after them. Even Enriquez is that way. And he thinks Jersey Slim is an unbeatable man. Because of his fierceness in battle and because of his hatred of all mankind."

Gunn smiled with satisfaction.

He slapped his knee, began to peel out of his shredded buckskins. He laid out his new clothes, good denims, dark shirt, socks. He cleaned and oiled his pistol, lay on the bed, the freshly loaded weapon close at hand.

"Let me sleep," he said. "An hour, hour and a half. Then wake me. I don't want to be to sluggish." The two girls giggled and said they would do that.

"No funny business," he warned. "I need all my sleep."

The girls restrained their titters, kept silent until they heard his heavy, even breathing. Then, they began whispering to themselves. After that, every so often, Junia went to the window, checked the angle of the sun. In this way, they kept track of the time. An hour and a half later, more or less, Junia nodded to Elena. Then, both girls slipped out of their dresses. Naked, they approached the bed from both sides. They looked at each other, at Gunn's still form, naked except for a pair of cheap floursack shorts, and winked at each other.

"Shhh!" warned Elena, sliding onto the bed beside Gunn.

Junia lay down on the other side.

Then, they began their devilish work.

Gunn wrestled with the dream.

He was being chased by faceless people through a thick field of thistles. The thistles scratched at his legs and arms. The plants twined around his wrists and he was being dragged by more people through the thistles. Then, his head struck a large stone which turned into a beehive. A swarm of bumble bees roared out of the hive, began pelting him on the face and neck. Stinging him. . . .

He awoke, felt the bee stings on his neck.

Only they weren't bee stings.

Kisses.

Bewildered, he tried to sit up. The room was dim, the shades tightly drawn.

He felt a naked breast. He reached out to the other side.

Another breast.

Laughter. Bright, musical. On both sides of him.

"Huh?" he said.

"Lie down, Gunn. You've slept. Almost two hours."

"We want to play with you a while," said another voice. Junia! And Elena!

Before he could say anything, he felt a hand in his groin. A soft hand closing around the lifeless muscle of his manhood.

Junia squeezed him. Elena leaned over, slithered her tongue inside his mouth. He felt a twinge of desire. His cock moved, hardening.

"Girls, girls. . . ."

"Hush," whispered Elena. "There's plenty of time. We want to share you. . . ."

"Share me?" Gunn husked weakly.

Junia's mouth on him, lathering his cock with saliva. Elena pushing her tongue inside his ear. Torture. Sheer torture.

But delicious. And maddening.

"You don't have to do anything," Elena said. "We will do it all."

It was so.

Gunn relaxed, made out their forms. All gentle curves, sweeping backs, clean sweet shoulders. Dark valleyed loins and soft breasts. Golden and tawney bodies, hands touching him in sensitive places. Toes sliding up and down his leg. Mouths at his groin, behind his ears, tongues tracking across his quivering belly. He cursed and smiled. He tingled all over.

"Who's first?" he asked, the fever in him great.

"Junia has the honors," said Elena, her mouth wet, her breasts heaving.

Gunn rose above the willing Junia, dipped between her spread-eagled legs. Sank into the steamed pudding of her sex-cleft. Elena's hand slid under his buttocks, grasped the thick base of his stalk, squeezed it. A fire-hot bolt of lightning shot up his spine.

Junia swallowed his manhood. He sank through lava-warm seas to the depths of her honey-pit. Soft hands brushed his back.

Elena stroked his cock when it was out of Junia's

sheath, slick with their love juices. She tenderly rubbed his buttocks, fondled his sac with delicate hands, kneading the testicles with exquisite care.

Junia flamed and spurted with orgasm. Clawed at his back without breaking the skin. Ice running along his spine. Fire in his loins. Madness in his brain. Sweetness in his belly.

"Now me," said Elena later.

He climbed atop her and Junia embraced them both as they humped away. Kissed him in delicate places. He seemed to be entangled in women. In their breasts, legs, thighs, bubbling crevices.

Elena burst, overflowed.

Again and again.

Then it was Junia. Then, Elena again until it no longer mattered.

But he gave Junia his seed.

A gracious act on Elena's part.

He thought.

Ten minutes later, they were at it again. Both of them. And, nothing left of him, he was sure.

But Elena took his seed.

The two women buried him in breasts and loving arms. Smothered him with kisses.

He struggled up out of the tangle.

The sun was falling in the sky.

It was time to go.

Time to meet Santos.

If he was there.

If not, he would kill him.

A sad thing, when there was so much love in the world. In the room. Now.

It was tough to leave.

"*Adios*," said Gunn. Finally, dressed and fit. Lean as a whip and raring to go. "I'll see you *mañana*, lord willing."

"We will miss you," chorused the girls.

"And I will not think of you at all," he said grimly, "or I'll surely die."

Their laughter rang in his ears like a horseshoe game as he closed the door.

EIGHTEEN

Santos was there.

Unarmed.

He slouched in a chair in the lobby of the hotel, rose to his feet as Gunn came down the stairs, carrying a bundle under his arms, a rifle in one hand.

"The horses are ready. So am I," Santos said simply.

Outside, Gunn spoke to him.

"You have my promise, Santos," Gunn said. "If you're square with me, I won't bother you. You're free to go after I make my play. Fair enough?"

Santos thought of the shadow. Gunn's shadow. The shadow that was not of the earth, but of the spirit. He had thought about that a lot in the time since Gunn had last spoken to him. It was a mystical thing. Men seldom spoke of the *sombra,* but he had listened to the old ones speak of it in Mexico after the Sonoran sun had set and when it was quiet on the plain. When the cactus threw long shadows and the nightbats flew. Some men had a shadow following them all of their lives. A shadow that protected them, made them strong. Gunn, he was sure, was such a man.

"I will not double the cross for you," Santos said. "Jersey Slim will shoot me on sight. Perhaps Enriquez too. I do not even ask for a gun, but if I had one I would help you."

Gunn believed him.

"I will buy you a rifle and pistol."

Santos grinned.

"There is no need. I have spares at the saloon. *La Copa de Oro*. If you will permit me, I will get them."

"Meet me at the livery," Gunn said, walking across the screet. His senses were fine-tuned. The dusk air had a liveliness to it that he had felt only a few times before. Santos had made his decision. He might prove to be a valuable ally.

Gunn looked at the sky.

There would be no bad weather. The clouds were high, feathered and the sky would turn red as the sun set, promising fair weather on the morrow. Swallows were flying high, catching insects on the wing. The smoke fires in the town rose straight up in the air. He hitched his belt with satisfaction, entered the livery.

The horses were saddled. The claybank gelding and Santos' horse.

There was no sign of Juan Cardona, which was just as well. Gunn did not want to have to explain anything to the man.

Santos arrived a few moments later, armed. He slid his rifle into its sheath, mounted up. Gunn would not need a rifle this night. His would be close work. There were times when a long gun was a handicap. He wanted his hands free. But the rifle was snug in its scabbard, the contents of the bundle distributed in the saddle bags. In the time he had waited for Santos, he had changed into a pair of moccasined boots. If he was afoot, he didn't want to break an ankle nor make a lot of undue noise. The clothes he wore fit him well, were comfortable.

"Ready?" he asked the Mexican.

"Pues, sí."

"Vamanos!"

The two men rode out the back of the livery, headed for the broken hills. Gunn had a pretty good idea of the location of Enriquez's camp. He let Santos ride slightly ahead and to his right. It wasn't necessary to mention this to Santos. He knew. The two men fell into a steady pace, the horses moving along with an easy rolling gait. Gunn had a plan in mind, but would wait until they were close before he divulged it to Santos. The less the man knew now, the better. He had sided with Gunn, but already Gunn knew him to be a flighty man, loyal only to his own whim.

The miles crept by, the sun sank over the western buttes. As Gunn had figured, the sky was red as blood, the sunset brilliant. Once the sun dropped from sight, the land was plunged into eerie shadows. The tall saguaros took on the shapes of men, the rocks became fortresses, places of ambush. Two hours after leaving town, Santos reined up.

"Do you know where we are?" he asked Gunn.

Gunn had watched the stars, marked their general direction. By his figuring, they were not far from Enriquez's stronghold. They had been riding west and slightly north.

"Should be up ahead, not more than two miles to the canyon entrance."

"Good. You are right. There will be guards, two at least."

Gunn figured four. Maybe six.

"And?"

"I can take one side, you the other."

Gunn's scalp bristled. A klaxon sounded a warning in his brain.

"No," he said quietly. "Here's the way we will do it. You will ride up as if alone. You will answer the challenge and ride close if you are passed without trouble."

"But. . . .I will be a sitting turtle."

"You will not. Do you have tobacco?"

"Yes. I bought it fresh in town."

"Give some to the guards. Wait until they light up. Joke with them. Gossip. I don't care. I want to see at least one of them before you pass by. I will shoot that man and that will be your signal to double back, back me up. Can you do that? Will you? I don't want any bullshit now, Santos. We're down to hard brush on this gather and I'd just as soon kill you now as to have you chaffer me when the shooting starts."

"I will do what you say, but they might wonder why I am hanging around."

"They won't wonder very long. Throw your tobacco up and tell 'em to keep it. They'll love your ass from that moment until judgment day."

"Judgment day?"

"When I read 'em chapter and verse."

The moon stayed behind the high clouds. Through the patches, the stars shimmered in deep black fields of space. At ground level, it was pitch. The men on the high ground would be at a disadvantage. Gunn was counting on it. He hadn't told Santos all of his plan. Just enough to get the ball rolling. One thing was sure. They couldn't take any prisoners. Every guard on that ledge would have to go down. And stay down.

Gunn followed Pedro's lead through the saguaro. Grudgingly, he had to admit that Santos was good. He could see in the dark. He pulled no tricks even though Gunn watched him closely, his hand close to his pistol. Finally, Santos pulled up again.

Gunn rode up to him.

"Just over the rise. They can see us good from up there."

"You still figure only two guards, Santos?"

"Maybe more."

"Yeah, like four."

Gunn could almost see him shrugging in the dark. If Elena was right, Enriquez had doubled, maybe tripled the guard.

"I guess four or five. Because they will all be plenty drunk in camp."

"All right. Can you take a couple of them? Any good friends or relatives up there?"

"No."

"They all have to go to the wall, Santos."

"They will run, some of them."

"Even those. No one gets away. Clear?"

Santos thought of Gunn and his shadow. He shivered, though the air was not chill.

"Clear," he said.

"I'm going to make a wide circle, on foot. You do your business after I've been gone about twenty minutes. I'll need that much time."

"You are not going straight in, then?"

"No. I don't want you to know where I am. But I'll stay out of your way. When one of them lights up, I'll open the ball."

"I understand," said Santos.

Gunn asked Santos to point out the direction of the canyon entrance and where the guards were likely to be one more time. He set the image in his head and then rode off, swinging wide to the left. When the silhouette of Santos was gone from view, he dismounted, tied up the claybank gelding. He put a feed bag on the horse's muzzle to keep him still. Then, quickly, he crossed in front of Santos to the right. The guards, he knew, would be congregated to the right of the entrance. He had to steal up close enough to have a vantage point, yet not be seen. A tall order.

His boot moccasins made no sound as he clambered through sand and rocks, hunching over to keep his profile low. When he thought he had gone far enough, he made another right angle and headed straight for the butte. He dashed silently from saguaro to saguaro, hid behind jumbles or rocks to listen for sounds. He counted off the minutes.

The mouth of the canyon yawned ahead, just to his left. He scanned the top of the butte for signs of the guards. The glint of moonlight on a rifle barrel, the silhouette of a hat, movement. Fifteen minutes had gone by. He hoped Santos knew how to keep track of time.

Gunn moved out, low hunched.

He stopped at a point where he could still see the top of the butte.

Low voices came to him.

Speaking Spanish.

So far, the tone carried no hint that the guards were unduly suspicious. Small talk. Not much of it, at that.

He looked for a place to set himself up. Time was running short. He had to be in position before Santos arrived at the entrance.

The next part was the trickiest.

Gun saw where the face of the butte trailed off. The guards' horses, he figured, must be on the other side of the entrance, hidden. That would also be the place where they had climbed up. But there was another way. One they wouldn't be watching. He ran in short spurts, listened after each dash.

The talking stayed at the same level as before. Only now he could hear them more clearly. They were telling dirty jokes.

Gunn found a talus slope just as the moon showed through a hole in the clouds. The slope was narrow, angled. He might make it up that way. With only three minutes left before Santos was due to arrive, Gunn started climbing. The footing was treacherous. He grabbed tiny spires of rock, pulled himself up. If he had guessed wrong, he wouldn't make it in time. His whole plan would be in jeopardy. The narrow cut widened, veered off, giving him a more level path. Hauling himself up the steep places three feet at a time, he puffed and panted his way to the top. It was fairly flat, but the rocky terrain gave him plenty of cover. He saw no one.

Still keeping low, he moved toward the muffled sound of voices.

Santos finished counting in his head.

Twenty minutes was a long, boring time.

Gunn was plenty smart and now he was out there, invisible. Well, he would keep his promise to the man and not doublecross him. It would be too dangerous now, anyway. The shadow was out there too.

Santos rode over the rise toward the mouth of the canyon. During the day, the signaling was done by heliograph. At night, they used a different method.

When he was close enough, Santos fished out a match.

He struck it on his saddle horn, tossed it into the air. The match flared, sputtered as it fell. It went out when it touched the ground. Santos had been careful not to look at it.

He watched the top of the butte, instead.

A match flew up in the air, fell like a shooting star.

Santos rode on in, conscious that several pairs of eyes were on him.

"*Hola!*" he called. "It is me, Pedro Santos."

"You got any whiskey, Santos?"

"Hell no! I got tobacco."

"Good!" called another. "We are running short. Did you hear about the raid?"

"Yes. In town. Was it rich?"

"Very rich. Enriquez has him a new plaything. She is a *china.*"

"*China,* eh? *Muy bien.* I have news for him."

Santos rode closer, made out shapes above him. He wondered where Gunn was. His hands were sweaty. He reached back in his saddlebag for the tobacco tin. Found it. It slippped off his grip as if greased. He clutched at it again, held it this time.

"Did you bring the Morgan girl?" asked a guard. It was Manuel Innocente. The others were two brothers he knew, Esteban and Fidel Lopez. Only three men so far had spoken to him. Maybe that's all that were there.

"No. She was shot."

Santos stopped, heard someone scrambling down toward him.

He tossed the can of tobacco at the man.

"Ayy! Good throw!"

Santos' heart sank. He recognized the bulk and voice of Alejandro Jurado. So, at least four guards! Men he knew. Men he had ridden with from the border to Colorado, from California to Kansas. He cursed his luck under his breath.

"Is there anyone inside the canyon?" he asked Alejandro.

"We are the guards. There are six of us bullshitting up here. You can pass clear to the party. We will get just as drunk as you in the morning. Unless you care to relieve one of us!"

"Hell no!" said Santos, forcing the bravado. "I have important news for *el jefe.*"

"Important news of the *putas* in Tres Piedras, no doubt!" said Manuel.

"There are no *putas* in Tres Piedras," joked Santos. "I made them all honest women."

Wild laughter from the top of the butte.

Gunn crawled over the edge, looked down.

He saw Santos sitting in the saddle. Saw the man scrambling back up with the tin of tobacco. Heard the crackle of papers. The *pong* of the airtight can being pried open. The rustle of tobacco spilling onto crimped papers.

Saw the shapes of five men. Then another, off to

210

one side. He sat with his rifle across his lap. There was always one, he thought. One who had senses a little keener than the others.

He would be the one he'd have to take out first.

Gunn reached down, slid his pistol slowly from the holster.

The murmur of obscene voices drifted up to him.

Santos began backing his horse imperceptibly.

Gunn's chest heaved with satisfaction. Santos was ready. He knew what to do.

The pistol floated out in front of him, all six chambers loaded. He slipped four other bullets out of his gunbelt, put them where he could get them in a hurry.

"Fosforo? Quien tiene fosforo?"

One of the Mexican guards was asking for a match. It would be his last request.

Gunn squeezed the trigger of his Colt slightly, thumbed back the hammer. The locking sear made no sound. He took aim on the man sitting with the rifle in his lap, rested the butt of his pistol on his left palm. He aimed slightly low, at the shoulder. That way he was sure of a body hit if he missed the brain. He brought the barrel up slightly, after it was aligned, figuring on a slight rise in the trajectory. Shooting downhill was tricky. It was even trickier in the dark. He would have only one set shot. After that, he'd have to free his left hand to fan the hammer back. He wanted to pump six shots into the bunch as fast as he could reload, then pick out any stragglers. They would be confused at first, shooting uphill. But they would see his fire flashes and could blow him to kingdom come if he presented any kind of target at all.

Gunn waited for one of the men to light the match.

Seconds ticked by.

Santos edged backwards. Gunn saw his right arm drop to his side, his hand disappear in the darkness next to his leg.

Santos was ready.

So was he.

"Hey, Santos, what are you doing down there?" called one of the guards.

Gunn felt his heart rise up in his throat. Stick there like a gob of strangling mucus.

The talk died away.

Gunn saw heads move toward Santos.

He sucked in a breath, started to squeeze the trigger. He'd have to go it now, endanger Santos, if the bunch of bandits got real suspicious. It was hell waiting it out.

"Why doesn't Santos say anything?" he wondered.

"Santos? You awake?"

Finally Santos answered.

"I got a loose cinch, Esteban," replied Santos. "I am not asleep. Be going in a minute."

Loud guffaws greeted Santos' reply.

The heart slid down Gunn's throat.

But the rifleman started to get up.

Just then, one of the men lit a match. The glow flared over the bronzed leather of his face.

Gunn's man was still moving, rising from his sitting position. His aiming would do him no good now.

He had to shoot.

His barrel followed the man.

The match went out just as Gunn fired.

The explosion seemed to rock the earth, splitting

212

eardrums, opening up the throats of enraged men.

The night erupted in more explosions, orange balls of fire, the whinewhistle of leaden bees, the awful curses of men caught by surprise.

And the terrible screams of men dying.

NINETEEN

Chunks of rock and grit stung Gunn's face.

Orange flowers of death blossomed below him. Out of the corner of his eye, he saw Santos firing. Heard the thunk of lead plunking into flesh. A man screamed and fell over the edge. His body crashed against rock, thudded when it hit the ground.

Gunn fanned his pistol, scooted behind a rock.

He picked out targets that were only shadows, brief silhouettes lit by the flame of gunfire.

Curses filled the air.

Gunn shot as fast as he could, then opened the cylinder gate on the Colt. He spun it, triggering the ejector rod as fast as he could. Found the four bullets, rammed them in the empty holes, pushing them in tightly with his thumb. Closed the gate, spun two spaces and cocked the hammer back full.

Rolled away as bullets fried the air over his head, sought him through sheared-off chunks of stone, in the tufts of grasses inches away.

The firing died down.

Gunn's eyes strained to see who was left down below.

Someone moved.

Gunn fired pointblank.

A man screamed in mortal pain.

The echoes of gunfire faded. The scream died out. The smell of burnt powder hung in the air.

Smoke wisps floated over the dead and the dying like shrouds.

"Santos. . . ." Gunn called softly.

"I am all right."

"Anybody get away?"

"Not this way."

"I'll have to go down there. Make a count. Cover me. . . ."

Gunn reloaded his pistol, sucked in a deep breath. He slipped over the edge of the tabletop, dropped to the floor of the outpost.

Listened.

The labored sound of a man struggling for breath reached his ears. Gunn hunched low, headed toward it.

A man sobbed.

Gunn heard the whisper of a prayer, a plea for forgiveness, absolution.

Then it was quiet.

Gunn counted the bodies, the stench of death thick in his nostrils.

"I count six," he said. The man with the rifle had been shot clean through the temple.

"That's all that were here," said Santos, his voice a hard rasp.

"I'm going to drop some things down to you. Catch them."

Gunn started checking the weapons in the dark. He

selected two of the new Sharps, carried them to the edge. Santos was waiting. He tossed one down at a time. The Mexican caught them. Gunn then found a man his size, stripped him out of his clothes. He took off his new duds and pulled on the dead man's clothes. Took a hat to replace his own. He filled his pockets with ammunition for the Sharps rifles.

"Meet me where they staked their horses," he told Santos. "I'm going to ride one of theirs into the camp."

The rifles clattered as Santos moved on into the canyon. Gunn picked his way down the trail, his heart still pounding in his chest. The air was sweeter below the killing place.

The trail wound down to a pocket in the canyon wall. Gunn carried the bundle of his new clothes. No use wasting them. When he dropped down to the place where the bandits' horses were picketed, Gunn looked like any one of a number of Mexican bandits. He wore the *bandaleros,* the *sombrero.* He still wore his own boot moccasins.

Santos swore.

"I almost shot you," he said. "I thought you were. . . ."

"That's good. Maybe Enriquez will think so too." Gunn grinned, a flash of white teeth in the dark. "Now. Any chance of those in camp hearing the gunfire?"

"Maybe. I don't think so. It is more than a mile in and the canyon winds around."

That's what Gunn had figured. The canyon would act as a baffle to kill the sound of fighting. Anyone listening carefully though probably could have heard the reports. They would not sound like rifle or pistol fire, but as far-off cracks or pops such as mountains and forests make when the night temperatures change.

"Which horse?" Gunn asked Santos.

"You look more like Esteban. Take his. The grulla."

Gunn mounted the rugged pony, reached for a Sharps. Checked the loads.

"Here's some ammunition for your rifle. Know how to work it?"

"I think so."

"Big gun for a big job," Gunn said. "Now, we'll run these other horses into camp, stir it up. What time do the guards change?"

"Just before dawn," said Santos. "That's when Enriquez also sends out his scouts."

"How many scouts?"

"Four or five."

"That's four or five less men to worry about. But we can't wait that long. I'm going to shoot every man I see and you do the same. We'll need to get to Morgan first, and see that we corner that ammunition dump. That's where the real fight will be if Enriquez is any kind of a soldier."

"He is. And I think you are right."

They gathered up the horses. Gunn took three of them, Santos the other two. Led them up the winding canyon. Gunn deliberately kept the pace slow, stopping every so often to listen.

Gunn was riding in blind. It was pitch dark in the canyon. Santos, just ahead, was picking his way, too. Overhead, the stars seemed fixed in the heavens and the moon had been swallowed up by thickening clouds. The horses' hooves made soft muffled metallic sounds in the dirt, following a trail only they could sense.

Before they got to the canyon itself, Gunn heard the sounds.

Like far-off gunshots.

Santos halted.

"They are shooting off their guns I think," he said, an uncertainty to his tone of voice.

"Maybe." Gunn wasn't convinced. The pops were close together as if a line of men were firing on command. A sound not unlike those battles in the War where men had lined up on both sides and fired at one another, the blue and the gray. "Wasting a lot of ammunition if so."

"What should we do?"

"Go on. They're busy anyway. Might work in our favor."

The canyon twisted once more and then opened to the wider, walled-in meadow where Enriquez made his camp.

As they came into the main canyon, Santos and Gunn looked up at the sky in awe. Their faces flickered with color.

Santos backed up his horse.

A rocket shot up into the sky, exploded into a shower of colorful sparks.

Cheers and shouting rose in the air from the camp.

More rockets went up, then another string of firecrackers.

"Fireworks!" said Gunn. "I'll be damned."

"Yes. Where did they get such wonders?"

"From today's raid, no doubt," said Gunn grimly. He stopped flinching every time a string of firecrackers went off. It was unnerving, but would work to his advantage, this spectacle.

"Now what?" asked Santos.

"Point out the place where they store the ammunition. Then show me where Morgan is kept. I want to get it straight in my mind."

Someone started running toward the two men.

Santos pointed to a place almost dead center in the meadow. "There's the cache," he said. He pointed to the huts and caves along the wall, counted. "There is where you will find Morgan."

The man kept running toward them.

Gunn dropped the reins of his horse and three others, slid the Sharps out of its sheath. It was as good a time as any to sight the weapon in. He raised the rifle to his shoulder, drew a bead on the running man. He dropped the barrel for lead, squeezed the trigger. The big Sharps boomed.

The running man threw up his arms, stumbled and pitched forward. He skidded on his belly, lay still, a puffcloud of dust hanging over him like a pall. Smoke from the rifle fanned out in layers.

"Now!" Gunn yelled, grabbing up his reins in one hand, wheeling the grulla. He circled the three horses he'd been leading, slapped their rumps with the rifle butt. They shot toward the camp. Santos slapped the two horses with him and they raced after the others.

A huge rocket flared over them and Gunn headed for the wall.

Orange flames blossomed from somewhere ahead and he heard the sing-whine of bullets ripping through the air. Santos veered off to his left, hugging his saddle, firing with his pistol.

Gunn reached the first lean-to, slid out of the saddle. He hit the ground running, saw the grulla take a hit, stagger, drop to its knees.

Men shouted and he heard a woman scream.

Gunshots pounded the walls of the canyon, echoing into thunderclaps.

Gunn hunched low, started picking targets. Shooting and reloading, he saw men fall. Still, he kept creeping down the line of huts, past the caves. Santos was firing from the center of the canyon, trying to work his way on foot to the ammo cache. Horses squealed in terror. Men grabbed some of them up and tried to ride him down. He emptied the saddles as fast as they came.

"Morgan?" Gunn called when he drew near the lean-to where rifles and pistols were stacked on tables under a canvas tarp.

"Over here! That you, Gunn?"

"Hold fast." Gunn slinked under the lean-to. A bullet slammed into the rifles. Wood and metal clattered together.

Morgan's head and shoulders rose out of the darkness.

"Got a rifle you can use?" Gunn asked.

"Dang sure! Man it's good to see you. These bandits been drinkin' and shootin' off firecrackers all damned night. Thought they was goin' to blow us all to smithereens.

"Gunn?"

A soft musical voice from somewhere behind Morgan.

"Yeah?"

"I prayed you would come. Do you not remember me?"

Gunn moved closer, fired off a shot at a man running on an angle toward a cave. The man went head over heels, fell with a *whump!*

"Who are you?" he asked, his breath whistling through his teeth.

A hand touched his arm. Morgan used the table as a bench rest, started firing the Sharps. A man screamed.

Gunn saw them now, in the brief flashes of light. A group of men huddled between the dwellings and the ammo cache. But they were backing up, circling, edging toward the ammunition. It was dark as the bowels of hell.

The voice at his ear was tinged with a faint accent. Somehow familiar to him.

"It is I, Soo Li."

He heard the rustle of silk. Felt a soft breast pressing against his forearm.

He remembered. The Mission Cataldo. Hop Chee and Ling. A long time ago. The beautiful Chinese girl.

"How. . . ?"

"We were bringing goods to Taos when these filthy bandits ambushed us. They captured me."

Gunn's jaw set in a hard line.

"Get down and out of the way," he told her. "It's going to be a long hard night."

"I am glad you are here." Her lips brushed across his cheek. He heard her move away, behind him.

Gunn moved up beside Ethan Morgan.

"How many out there?" he asked.

"Less than a dozen I reckon."

The firing died down. Enriquez rallied his men. Gunn heard him bark orders.

"We got much ammunition here?"

"Not much. Eva. . . ."

"She's all right. Took a bullet in the leg. Someone's taking right good care of her."

"Thank God."

There was a pounding of hoofbeats. Gunn looked up, saw dark shadows racing away.

"Cowards," muttered Ethan.

He was right, Gunn figured. Some of Enriquez's men were running away. He let them go. There was no use wasting ammunition on men who were beaten. He could not see how many were left, but he heard noise, detected movement out there.

Another man rode off and Gunn realized his mistake when he heard Enriquez shout: *Andale!*

"Damn!" he said. "Those men aren't running away. Enriquez sent them! They're going after help— or. . . ." He didn't finish the sentence. No use to alarm Morgan. He had to admire Enriquez though. He didn't miss a trick.

"Three men, I count," said Morgan.

"Too late now. Let's take stock."

Gunn counted the shells in his *bandaleros*. Morgan counted up his remaining ammunition.

"Forty rounds for me," said Gunn.

"A dozen I have."

"Pick your shots. Anybody rushes us, shoot. Anybody mounts up, drop him."

But there was no more firing.

"Gunn? You wall-eyed bastard, I'll get you!"

There was no mistaking the voice.

Jersey Slim Norris!

Gunn said nothing.

"Morgan! You too! I'll cut your balls off and feed 'em to you."

222

Mexicans began shouting insults. The insults cut to the bone. Gunn put an arm on Morgan.

"Don't pay any attention to them. They're trying to rattle you."

The Mexicans were describing his daughter's anatomy and love life in filthy, disgusting terms. The English was bad, but understandable.

"They must be low on ammunition too."

"Why don't they go to the cache?" asked Morgan.

One of them tried it. A shot rang out from the other side.

Gunn grinned in the dark.

"Because Santos is out there, holding them off."

His grin faded when he realized that Santos couldn't have much ammunition left either. The shot had come from his pistol, not the Sharps.

A flutter of shots boomed as bandits tried to shoot Santos.

Gunn watched the fire flashes, saw that the bandits had made a half-circle on the cache.

Santos fired again. The Sharps this time. A man screamed in agony as his shot hit home.

Now Gunn knew where everyone was, just about.

Santos was on the other side of the cache, using it for cover. To the right, Enriquez and his men lay in darkness, unable to reach the ammunition without paying in blood.

Every move they made toward the ammunition cost them hard bullets as well.

Bullets that were running out.

"Now what?" asked Soo Li, venturing closer to the two men under the lean-to.

"We wait," said Gunn quietly. "Until dawn. We

can't sleep, but neither can they. We have to listen and mistrust every sound."

"It's a nightmare," said Soo Li.

"Yes. The dark is fearful at times."

"I'm not afraid. With you here."

Her arms twined around his waist.

He felt her shudder against his back.

There was no time for her now. But he remembered her.

"Did. . . .did Enriquez. . . ." he started to ask.

Then he heard her sobbing and knew the answer.

He turned, kissed her.

"The nightmare will be over in a few hours," he said. "Don't think about him."

"Kill him," she hissed. "Kill him dead, Gunn."

"I will," he promised.

TWENTY

The night was long and dangerous.

Ethan Morgan fell asleep, hunched over the Freund Sharps.

Gunn heard his soft snoring.

Soo Li lay huddled at Gunn's feet, dozing.

Gunn's senses prickled at every sound, every hint of movement from the meadowed canyon floor. A horse whickered. A cock owl growled. A man coughed. Another, wounded, groaned.

Towards dawn, Gunn fought to stay awake.

He heard a sound that was like no other. Separate, distinct. But elusive. He peered into the blackness, then closed his eyes. The strain was too great. When he opened them again, the darkness seemed deeper, more intense. An ink sea floating at the shore of the lean-to, hemming him in, smothering him with the coils of claustrophobia.

The sound was faint, sporadic.

A whisper of cloth. A scratch of boot. Silence. A breath sucked in, let out slow.

Gunn waited patiently, squinting in the dark, in the

direction of the almost soundless sound.

Someone was creeping, crawling toward the lean-to. An expert. Taking his time.

Gunn tried to judge the distance.

Impossible, almost. Every time he locked onto the sound, it faded. The silence was agonizing. Morgan's light snoring interfered with Gunn's hearing. Soo Li whimpered in dream and his senses jerked.

The sound stopped for a long time.

Gunn listened to his own breathing. His ears strained harder to pick up the faintest noise. His heart pounded with fear. The man could be behind him, in front of him, crawling under the table, knife in hand! The man could be waiting a few yards away for first light, ready to shoot — and kill!

Was the man that patient?

Gunn made no move. His nose itched. He did not scratch it. His left hand began to tingle as the blood circulation slowed. He dared not flex his hand to restore the blood flow. He was stone. Only his hand on the Sharps was relaxed, the trigger finger loose in the trigger guard. Ready.

Hours seemed to go by. Centuries. Eternities.

Still, there was no detectable sound.

The silence was maddening.

Soo Li stirred and Gunn's nerves rattled like the seeds in shook gourds.

Morgan groaned in sleep. His snoring stopped abruptly.

Still, Gunn did not move.

He waited, his breath hot in his chest. His chest heavy as lead.

The sky began to lighten.

The air seemed filled with pale smoke. Then, a finger of light etched itself on the skyline of the canyon walls.

The Mexican rose up from the darkness, both hands filled.

Two pistols roared pointblank.

From the bunch out on the flats, a hail of gunfire erupted, perfectly timed.

Withering fire laced through the lean-to, snapping at rifles, wood posts, canvas, spanging off of rock walls. The angry lethal whine of lead filled the close pre-dawn air.

Gunn shoved the Sharps out straight, pulled the trigger.

Smoke and flame belched from the end of the barrel. The Mexican took the heavy slug in his chest. He staggered back, pistols still smoking, a flowering red stain spreading from the hole in his breastplate.

Ethan snatched up his rifle, began firing into the smoke.

Soo Li cried out, scrambled for cover with a rustle of silk. Gunn saw wide, fear-filled eyes under heavy black bangs.

Bullets poured into the lean-to, whizzing like angered bees.

Through the smoke, Gunn saw that only two or three men were still shooting out near the ammunition boxes. It was then that he noticed they were being fired on from another direction. Beyond the cluster of men, fire blasts came from a small outcropping of rocks, perhaps fifty yards behind.

Pedro Santos shot one of the men near the ammo pile.

Morgan shot another.

Santos stood up, charged the remaining man who wheeled and grabbed for his pistol. Santos shot him in his tracks. He gave a jubilant cry.

"Look out!" Gunn shouted, trying to warn Santos that he was exposed to deadly fire from behind the outcropping.

Santos stopped. A rifle cracked. A puff of smoke sped from behind the rocks, fanned by orange flame.

"Christ!" exclaimed Gunn.

Santos danced as the bullet caught him in the forehead. His legs seemed galvanized as he staggered about like a beheaded chicken. His rifle fell from his grasp and he hopped in a circle before crumpling to the ground, stone dead.

It was quiet.

Soo Li peered from behind an empty rifle crate.

"Are they all dead?"

"No," said Gunn. "I've got five shots left. How about you, Morgan?"

"One in the chamber."

"Someone's over there behind those rocks. At least two men." Gunn had a hunch who they were. Sometime during the night while the one Mexican was crawling toward the lean-to, Enriquez and Jersey Slim had gone off at an angle, holing up in the rocks. The execution was perfectly timed. Gunn had to admire Enriquez' strategy. By all rights, he and Morgan should have been killed in the first volley. The fact that Morgan had been asleep probably saved his life. And Soo Li had been lying low. Gunn had been ready for the lone charging man. Still, they got caught in withering crossfire and if the marksmanship had been better. . . .

"What now?" asked Morgan.

"I'll have to try and make it to the ammo. Santos is dead. There's only you and me. I think Enriquez must be low on bullets too. It's going to be a race."

As if to punctuate his words, another shot rang out.

The heavy Sharps bullet smashed into Ethan's rifle, snatching it from his hands. The bullet hit the stock, but it was dangerously close. Splinters of wood knifed into Morgan's elbow. He cried out in pain.

Gunn saw movement, fired.

Four shots left.

"Can you still use the rifle?" Gunn asked.

Morgan picked it up, brushed away splinters from the hole in the stock.

"Yes," he replied.

"Give it to me and you take this one. I'm going out to see if I can get us some more ammunition."

"You want me to cover you?"

"Just keep them honest over there."

Gunn took Morgan's rifle, ducked under the table. He crawled to the Mexican he had just killed, used him for cover. Bullets fried the air over his head. He ate dirt.

Soo Li screamed.

Gunn ignored her. He stuck a boot out. A shot furrowed the earth near his heel.

Whoever was shooting at him was a marksman!

Gunn turned at a sound behind him.

Hoofbeats!

"My God, it's Eva!" yelled Morgan.

Gunn fired the last round in the Sharps, dashed back to cover.

Morgan was right. One of the Mexicans who had

escaped the night before had Eva Morgan in front of him. He rode around the ammo boxes to a point between the outcropping and where Gunn, Morgan and Soo Li were holed up.

The horseman stopped.

He held a knife to Eva's throat.

Gunn looked at her closely. She was pale, her bandage was bloody. Her skirt was up around her waist, her legs exposed. She appeared to be about to fall except that she was held fast by the bandit.

Out of the corner of his eye, Gunn saw Jersey Slim and Enriquez come out from behind the rock outcropping.

"It's all over, Gunn!" shouted Slim. "You're hog meat now!"

"He's right!" echoed Enriquez. "Throw down your weapons. We will not hurt any of you, I promise."

"In a pig's ass," Gunn muttered.

"What?" asked Morgan, bewildered by the odd turn of events.

"Nothing. I guess we better throw down our weapons."

"Surrender?"

"Yes, surrender."

"No!" Soo Li hissed. "You can't trust that bandit! He'll kill us all. Fight him, Gunn. Fight him to your last breath."

"If he hurts Eva, I'll. . . ." Morgan said, rising to aim the rifle at the bandit holding his daughter hostage.

Gunn wrestled the rifle away from Morgan, tossed it out in plain sight.

"You got the hand!" Gunn called out. "Turn the girl loose!"

To Morgan, he said: "Take my pistol, shove it in my belt, behind my back."

Morgan stepped in front of Gunn, slipped the pistol free, then stepped behind him. He lifted the shirt, shoved the pistol in the waistband so that it nestled in the small of Gunn's back.

The bandit rode up closer, his horse prancing. Bold, confident that he had won, he was grinning from ear to ear.

"We're unarmed!" Gunn said. "We're coming out!"

He lifted his hands up in surrender. Ethan followed suit.

"You stay put, Soo Li," Gunn said, *sotto voce.*

Gunn stepped out from under the lean-to, Morgan behind him.

They stood there, as Slim and Enriquez started walking toward them. Still wary, they held their rifles up chest-high.

A shot rang out.

No one expected it. Gunn saw no smoke. Instinctively, he dove for the ground. Morgan stood there, shock on his face.

Slim and Enriquez threw themselves face down into the dirt, too rattled to fire.

Gunn looked at Eva, the bandit.

The bandit stared blankly into space. His hand loosened, the knife fell free. The horse reared. The bandit fell off sideways, a hole in his back. Eva landed on top of the ammunition cache.

Gunn didn't wait.

He reached up, rifle to his shoulder.

Gunn shot him once, twice, a third time. Each shot rammed home. The first one caught Slim in the gut, just below his belt buckle. The second slammed into his heart. The last one blew a black hole right between his eyes. Gunn fanned the hammer, controlled the bucking Colt by sheer muscle and determination. Slim did a little dance of death and his legs went out from under him. He fell in front of Enriquez, who hugged the ground.

"Eva, throw me a box of Sharps ammunition!" Gunn shouted. "Quick!"

Gunn whirled, fired at the Mexican's horse. The animal dropped like a stone. The tall, gray-eyed man raced to it as Enriquez began to fire his own Sharps. A bullet tugged at Gunn's borrowed hat. He dove the last six feet to land behind the heart-shot horse. He hated to kill a good animal like that, but the horse was his only cover. Out in the open, the long gun in Enriquez's hands would have shot him to rags.

Eva fumbled through the boxes, trying to find what Gunn was after. She knew her father's goods, finally found a box of Sharps ammunition. Gunn reached out, pulled in the emptied rifle as Enriquez's rifle boomed again. Dirt stung Gunn's wrist, but he retrieved the weapon.

"Here!" Eva cried with joy, "I found it!"

She tossed the box to Gunn. He emptied half of it on the ground.

"Get ready, Ethan!" Gunn called. He lay on his back, took aim. He hurled the box to Ethan under the lean-to. He caught it in one hand.

Gunn reloaded the Sharps with the shot-up stock. His hands were slick with sweat.

Eva lay exposed atop the ammo pile.

Apparently Enriquez noticed it at the same time as

Gunn. His next shot slammed into the boxes, showering Eva with splinters of wood. Gunn fired the Sharps until the barrel was hot and it was empty. Then he crawled toward Eva. Enriquez didn't fire. Gunn covered the girl with his body, reloaded the Sharps and his pistol during the lull. Ethan began firing at Enriquez who was using Slim's body for cover.

Gunn waited.

He saw the snout of the Sharps barrel poke over Slim's chest. The barrel spewed forth smoke and flame.

Gunn returned fire. So did Ethan.

Then he saw a handkerchief waving in the air behind Slim's body.

"I am out of ammunition!" cried Enriquez. "Don't shoot any more."

Gunn waited to see if the man was playing one last trick.

Finally, he replied.

"Stand up, raise your hands in the air. One false move and we drop you, Enriquez."

Enriquez stood up. He raised his hands high. They were empty.

"Start walking this way," ordered Gunn.

Enriquez walked toward him. Gunn stood up, holding only the Colt. Enriquez was close enough. Gunn watched him carefully. There was a noise behind him. More hoofbeats.

His heart sank.

"Eva!" he said, "grab the Sharps. Shoot if it's more bandits.

"It isn't!" she cried. "It's Elena and Junia. They must have shot. . . ."

Gunn half turned.

It was true. Elena and Junia were astride horses, galloping toward them from the canyon entrance.

Enrico kept coming until he was close to Gunn.

Gunn shoved his pistol in his waistband as the two girls rode up.

"We killed the bandit who had Eva!" said Junia. "Elena did. We killed two more too! You have done it, Gunn. You have killed Slim and you have captured Enriquez!"

Her joy was short-lived.

Gunn reached out for Enriquez.

Enriquez dropped his hand, pulled out a concealed dagger. He lunged for Gunn, slashing with the knife.

Gunn sidestepped, grabbed his wrist.

He twisted, pushed.

The dagger buried itself in Enriquez's gut. His eyes went wide in surprise. Blood poured from his mouth. Gunn wrenched the dagger free. Enriquez's hands went to his stomach. Blood gushed over his fingers. He crumpled in a heap, his eyes pleading for a mercy that was not there.

Soo Li rushed out of hiding, came up and threw her arms around Gunn.

Eva stood up, brushed herself off.

Ethan strode over, put his arm around Eva, hugged her tightly.

"It's by God over," he breathed.

"Yes," said Gunn, "it's over."

★　★　★

"I reckon I'll ride into town with you and Eva, Ethan, then go to the fair with you. We'll get some help loading the wagons out here. You and Soo Li ought to do pretty good considering."

"We might do fair at that," said Ethan.

"I—I don't know," said Soo Li. "They have shot up most of the fireworks. But there are beads and games that I might sell."

"Can we come along too?" asked Elena.

"Yes, we can help!" said Junia.

"Sure," said Gunn, grinning. "The more the merrier."

"I don't know if that's such a good idea," said Eva Morgan, frowning.

"You want to sell rifles, don't you? These two gals would make pretty good drummers."

"And pretty good. . . ."

"Don't say it, Eva," Gunn warned.

Then he took her in his arms, kissed her. She clung to him. He could hear her heartbeat.

"I guess I'm just being selfish, aren't I?" she whispered. "But you're not selfish, are you, Gunn?"

"Not a damned bit," admitted Gunn, his smile wide. "Always did believe in sharing what you got plenty of."

Gunn helped Eva walk to a wagon. She limped along, favoring her hurt leg.

Soo Li looked at the other two girls, strangers.

"Do you believe in sharing?" she asked.

Elena glowered at her. Junia pouted.

"Well, you'd better," said the Chinese beauty, "because I've known Gunn a long time. And I've missed him. If you give me any trouble, I'll just scratch your eyes out."

Gunn looked back over his shoulders at the three

girls squaring off.

"None of that," he said. "One wounded is enough. We've got a long ride ahead and unto everything there is a season."

"Bible stuff," snorted Ethan.

"Common sense," said Gunn. "It's hard enough to get along with one woman, let alone three or four."

"You got a point, Gunn."

And Gunn knew that everything was going to be just fine. For everyone.

ADVENTURES OF A SOLDER OF FORTUNE:
by Axel Kilgore

THEY CALL ME THE MERCENARY #1:   (678, $2.25)
THE KILLER GENESIS

Hank Frost, the one-eyed mercenary captain, wages a war of vengeance against a blood-crazy renegade commander!

THEY CALL ME THE MERCENARY #2:   (719, $2.25)
THE SLAUGHTER RUN

Assassination in the Swiss Alps . . . terrorism in the steaming Central American jungle . . . treachery in Washington . . . and Hank Frost right in the middle!

THEY CALL ME THE MERCENARY #3:   (753, $2.25)
FOURTH REICH DEATH SQUAD

Frost must follow the bloody trail of sadistic neo-Nazi kidnappers, himself pursued by a beautiful agent who claims to be their victim's daughter!

THEY CALL ME THE MERCENARY #4:   (809, $2.25)
THE OPIUM HUNTER

Frost penetrates the Siamese jungle in a campaign against vicious drug warlords—and finds himself up to his eyepatch in trouble!

THEY CALL ME THE MERCENARY #5:   (829, $2.50)
CANADIAN KILLING GROUND

Protecting a seven-year-old genius turns out much harder for Frost than he thought. He gets trapped between the Mounties and the PLO, and there's no way out!

WORLD WAR II
FROM THE GERMAN POINT OF VIEW

SEA WOLF #1: STEEL SHARK   (755, $2.25)
by Bruno Krauss
The first in a gripping new WWII series about the U-boat war waged in the bitter depths of the world's oceans! Hitler's crack submarine, the U-42, stalks a British destroyer in a mission that earns ruthless, ambitious Baldur Wolz the title of "Sea Wolf"!

SEA WOLF #2: SHARK NORTH   (782, $2.25)
by Bruno Krauss
The Fuhrer himself orders Baldur Wolz to land a civilian on the deserted coast of Norway. It is winter, 1940, when the U-boat prowls along a fjord in a mission that could be destroyed with each passing moment!

SEA WOLF #3: SHARK PACK   (817, $2.25)
by Bruno Krauss
Britain is the next target for the Third Reich, and Baldur Wolz is determined to claim that victory! The killing season opens and the Sea Wolf vows to gain more sinkings than any other sub in the Nazi navy . . .

SEA WOLF #4: SHARK HUNT   (833, $2.25)
by Bruno Krauss
A deadly accident leaves Baldur Wolz adrift in the Atlantic, and the Sea Wolf faces the greatest challenge of his life—and maybe the last!

Available wherever paperbacks are sold, or order direct from the Publisher. Send cover price plus 50¢ per copy for mailing and handling to Zebra Books, 475 Park Avenue South, New York, N.Y. 10016. DO NOT SEND CASH.

THE DYNAMIC NEW WARHUNTER SERIES

THE WARHUNTER #1: KILLER'S COUNCIL   (729-5, $1.95)
by Scott Siegel
Warfield Hunter and the Farrel gang shoot out their bloody feud
in the little town of Kimble, where War Hunter saves the sheriff's
life. Soon enough, he learns it was a set-up—and he has to take on
a whole town singlehandedly!

THE WARHUNTER #2: GUNMEN'S GRAVEYARD
                                          (743-0, $1.95)
by Scott Siegel
When War Hunter escapes from the Comanches, he's stuck with
a souvenir—a poisoned arrow in his side. The parched, feverish
man lying in the dust is grateful when he sees two men riding his
way—until he discovers he's at the mercy of the same bandits who
once robbed him and left him for dead!

THE WARHUNTER #3:
THE GREAT SALT LAKE MASSACRE   (785-6, $2.25)
by Scott Siegel
War Hunter knew he was asking for trouble when he let lovely
Ella Phillips travel with him. It wasn't long in coming, and when
Hunter took off, there was one corpse behind him. Little did he
know he was headed straight for a rampaging band of hotheaded
Utes!

*Available wherever paperbacks are sold, or order direct from the
Publisher. Send cover price plus 50¢ per copy for mailing and
handling to Zebra Books, 475 Park Avenue South, New York,
N.Y. 10016. DO NOT SEND CASH.*

YOU WILL ALSO WANT TO READ . . .